BETROTHED:
TO THE
PEOPLE'S PRINCE

BETROTHED: TO THE PEOPLE'S PRINCE

BY

MARION LENNOX

MILLS & BOON®

First published in Great Britain 2009
Large Print edition 2010
Harlequin Mills & Boon Limited,
Eton House, 18-24 Paradise Road,
Richmond, Surrey TW9 1SR

© Marion Lennox 2009

ISBN: 978 0 263 21184 9

Harlequin Mills & Boon policy is to use papers that are
natural, renewable and recyclable products and made
from wood grown in sustainable forests. The logging and
manufacturing process conform to the legal environmental
regulations of the country of origin.

Printed and bound in Great Britain
by CPI Antony Rowe, Chippenham, Wiltshire

CHAPTER ONE

INTO her crowd of beautiful people came…Nikos.

She was taking a last visual sweep of the room, noting descriptions for tomorrow's fashion column.

The men were almost uniformly in black—black T-shirts, black jeans and designer stubble. The women were Audrey Hepburn clones. Cinched waists, wide skirts and pearls. The fifties look was now.

There was little eating. Cinched waists and 'body slimmers' didn't allow for snacking, the waiters were sparse and it wasn't cool to graze.

Nikos was holding a beer, and as the waiter passed with a tray of tiny caviar-loaded blinis he snagged four. He tipped one into his mouth, then turned back to search the room.

For her.

After all these years, he could still stop her world.

She'd forgotten to breathe. It was important to breathe. She took a too-big sip of her too-dry Martini and it went down the wrong way.

Uh-oh. If it wasn't cool to eat, it was even more uncool to choke.

But help was at hand. Smooth and fast as a panther, Nikos moved through the crowd to be by her side in an instant. He took her drink, slapped her back with just the right amount of force, and then calmly waited for her to recover.

Nikos.

She could faint, she thought wildly. An ambulance could take her away and she'd be in a nice, safe emergency room. Safe from the man she'd walked away from almost ten years ago.

But fainting took skills she didn't have. No one seemed about to call for help. No one seemed more than politely interested that she was choking.

Except Nikos.

She didn't remember him as this big. And this…gorgeous? He was wearing faded blue jeans instead of the designer black that was de rigueur in this crowd. His shirt was worn white cotton, missing the top two buttons. He had an ancient leather jacket slung over his arm.

The fashion editor part of her was appreciative. Nice.

More than nice. Nikos.

She coughed on, more than she needed to, trying desperately to give herself space. His dark hair was curly, unruly and a bit too long. His brown-black eyes were crinkled at the edges, weathered from a life at sea. Among this crowd of fake tans, his was undeniably real. His whole body was weathered by his work.

Nikos. Fisherman.

Her childhood love.

He'd grown from a gorgeous boy into a…what? She didn't have words to describe it. She was the fashion editor of one of the world's leading glossies, and she was lost for words.

Words were what she needed. She had to think of something to say. Anything. Almost every eye in the room was on them now. She couldn't retreat to choking again.

'You want your drink back?' His tone was neutrally amused. Deeper than last time she'd heard him. A bit gravelly, with a gorgeous Greek accent.

Sexy as hell.

He was balancing his beer, her Martini and his three remaining blinis. He'd used his spare hand to thump her.

He was large and capable and…

Nikos.

Now she'd stopped choking, the crowd had turned their attention to him. Well, why wouldn't they? The models, designers, media and buyers were openly interested. Maybe more than interested. Their concentrated attention contained more than a hint of lust.

'You going to live?' Nikos asked mildly, and she thought about it. She might. If he went away.

'What are you doing here?'

'Looking for you.'

'It's invitation only.'

'Yep,' he said, as if that hadn't even crossed his mind as something to bother about. How had he done it? People would kill for an invitation to this launch. He'd simply walked in.

'You look cute,' he said, raking her from head to toe.

Right. She'd gone to some trouble with her outfit. Her tiny red skirt was clinging in the right places, she'd managed to make her unruly black curls stay in a knot that was almost sophisticated, but in this crowd of fashion extremists she knew she disappeared.

'Go away,' she said, and he shook his head.

'I can't do that, Princess.'

'Don't call me that.'

'It's what you are.'

'Please, Nikos, not here.'

'Whatever,' he said easily. 'But we need to talk. Phones don't work. You keep hanging up.'

'You don't hang up phones any more.' Very knowledgeable, she thought. What sort of inane talk was this?

'On Argyros we hang up telephones. After we talk to people.'

'I don't live on Argyros.'

'Yeah, that's what I want to talk to you about. It's time you came home.' He handed her back her Martini. He drained his beer and ate his three bite-sized blinis, then looked about for more. Two waiters were beside him in an instant.

He always had been charismatic, Athena thought. People gravitated to him.

She'd gravitated to him.

'So how about it?' he said, smiling his thanks to the waiters. Oh, that smile…

'Why would I want to come home?'

'There's the little matter of the Crown. I'm thinking you must have read the newspapers. Your cousin, Demos, says he's talked to you. I'm thinking Alexandros must have talked to you as well—or did you hang up on him, too?'

'Of course I didn't.'

'So you do know you're Crown Princess of Argyros.'

'I'm not Crown Princess of anything. Demos can have it,' she said savagely. 'He wants it.'

'Demos is second in line. You're first. It has to be you.'

'I have the power to abdicate. Consider me abdicated. Royalty's outdated and absurd, and my life's here. So, if you'll excuse me…'

'Thena, you don't have a choice. You have to come home.'

Thena. He was the only one who'd ever shortened her name. It made her feel…as she had no business feeling.

Just tell it like it is and move on, she told

herself. Be blunt and cold and not interested. He was talking history. Argyros was no longer anything to do with her.

'You're right,' she managed. 'I don't have a choice. My life is here.'

But not in this room. All of a sudden the room was claustrophobic. Her past was colliding with her present, and it made her feel as if the ground was shaking underneath her.

She and Nikos in the same room? No, no, no.

She and Nikos in the same city? She and Nikos *and their son?*

No!

Fear had her almost frozen.

'Nikos, this is futile,' she managed. 'There's no use telling me to go home. My home is here. Meanwhile, I have things to attend to, so if you'll excuse me…' She handed her Martini glass back to him and, before he could respond she swivelled and made her way swiftly through the crowd.

She reached the door—and she kept on walking.

She hadn't retrieved her checked coat. It didn't matter. Outside was cold, but she wasn't feeling cold. Her face was burning. She was shaking.

Maybe he'd let her be.

Or maybe not. He hadn't come all the way from Argyros to be ignored.

It was raining. Her stilettos weren't built for walking. She wanted to take them off and run. Because of course he'd follow.

Of course he did.

When he fell in step beside her she felt as if she'd been punched. Nikos… He threatened her world.

'Where are we going?' he asked mildly.

'Nowhere you're welcome.'

'Is this any way to greet family?'

'I'm not your family.'

'Tell that to my mother.'

His mother… She thought of Annia and felt a stab of real regret. She glanced sideways at Nikos—and then looked swiftly away. Annia… Argyros…

Nikos.

She'd walked away from them ten years ago. Leaving had broken her heart.

'It's your heritage,' he said mildly, as if he was simply continuing the conversation from back at the fashion launch.

'I never had a heritage. It was all about Giorgos.'

'The King's dead, Athena. He died without an heir. You know that.'

'And that makes a difference how?'

'It means the Diamond Isles become three Principalities again. The original royal families can resume rule. But you know this. By the way—did you also know that you're beautiful?' And he took her arm and forced her to stop.

She'd been striding. Angry. Fearful. Confused. Rain was turning to sleet. Her heels, her tight skirt and sheer pashmina wrap were designed for cocktail hour, not for street wear.

She should keep going but she wasn't all that sure where to go. She couldn't outwalk Nikos and she surely wasn't leading him back to her apartment. She surely wasn't leading him to her son.

She might as well stop. Get it over with now.

She turned to face him. A blast of icy wind hit full on, and she felt herself shudder.

Nikos's ancient leather jacket was suddenly around her, warm from his body, smelling of old leather and Nikos and…home. Argyros. Fishing boats in an ancient harbour. White stone villas hugging island cliffs. Sapphire seas and brilliant sun. The Diamond Isles.

Suddenly, stupidly, she wanted to cry.

'We need to get out of this,' Nikos said. His hand was under her elbow and he was steering her into the brightly lit portico of a restaurant, as if this was his town and he wasn't half a world away from where he lived and worked.

Nikos…

'You call those clothes?' he growled, and she remembered how bossy he'd been when they were kids, and how he was always right.

Bossy and arrogant and…fun. Pushing her past her comfort zone. Daring her to join him.

The number of times she'd ended up with skinned knees, battered and bruised because: 'Of course we can get up that cliff; you're not going to sit and watch like some *girl*, are you?'

She never did sit and watch. Even when they'd been older and the boys from the other islands became part of their pack, she'd always been included. Until…

Let's not go there, she told herself. She'd moved on. She was fashion editor for one of the world's best-selling magazines. She lived in New York and she was fine.

So what was Nikos doing, here, ushering her

into a restaurant she recognised? This place usually involved queuing, or a month or more's notice. But Nikos was a man who turned heads, who waiters automatically found a place for, because even if they couldn't place him they felt they should. He was obviously someone. He always had been, and his power hadn't waned one bit.

Stunned to speechlessness, she found herself being steered to an isolated table for two, one of the best in the house. The waiter tried to take her jacket—his jacket—but she clung. It was dumb, but she needed its warmth. She needed its comfort.

'What's good?' Nikos asked the waiter, waving away the menu.

'Savoury? Sweet?'

'Definitely something sweet,' he said, and smiled across the table at her. 'The way the lady's feeling right now, we need all the sugar we can get.'

She refused to smile back. She couldn't allow herself to sink into that smile.

'Crêpes?' the waiter proffered. 'Or if you have time…our raspberry soufflé's a house speciality.'

'Crêpes followed by soufflé for both of us then,' he said easily, and the waiter beamed and nodded and backed away, almost as if he sensed he shouldn't turn his back on royalty.

Nikos. Once upon a time…

No. Get a grip.

'I'm not going anywhere,' she muttered into the silence. 'You can't make me go back.'

Nikos smiled again—his smile wide and white, his eyes deep and shaded, an automatic defence against the sun. His smile was a heart stopper in anyone's language. Especially hers.

'You're right. I can't make you. You need to decide yourself. But that's why I'm here—to help you to decide that you need to come home.'

'My home's here.'

'Your career until now has been here,' he agreed. 'You've done very well.'

'There's no need to sound patronising.'

'I'm not patronising.'

'Like you'd know about my career.'

He raised his brows, half mocking. 'There were seven candidates for the position you're now in,' he said softly. 'Each of them was older, more experienced. You won the job over all of them and your boss believes he made a brilliant decision.'

'How do you know…'

'I've made it my business to find out.'

'Well, butt out. There's no need…'

'There is a need. There was always a chance that you'd inherit, and now you have.'

'I have no intention of inheriting. Demos wants it. Demos can have it. It should be you, but if that's not possible… Demos.'

'It was never going to be me.'

'You're nephew to the King.'

'You know the score,' he said evenly. 'Yes, my mother was the King's sister, but the King's lineage has to be direct and male. That's me out. But the individual island crowns have male/female equality. First in line for the throne of Argyros is you. Princess Athena, Crown Princess of Argyros. Sounds good, hey?' He smiled and tried to take her hand across the table. She snatched it away as if he burned.

'This is crazy. I've told you, Nikos, I'm not coming home.'

'Can I ask why not?'

'I don't belong there.'

'Of course you do. My family has always welcomed…'

'Your family,' she interrupted flatly. 'Of course. How's your wife?'

Why had she asked that? What possible difference did it make? But suddenly—she had to know.

Nikos didn't answer directly. He'd given up trying to take her hand. Instead he'd clasped his hands loosely on the table top. He flexed them now, still linked. Big hands and powerful.

He wasn't wearing a wedding ring.

She shouldn't even care. She shouldn't have asked.

But she had asked, and there was something in his face that said the answer was never going to be easy. For a couple of moments she thought he wouldn't answer at all. But finally he beckoned a waiter, ordered a beer and answered.

'Marika and I are divorced. She's remarried and left the island.' His gaze was expressionless, not giving a clue if this still had the power to hurt.

Ten years ago—two months after she'd left the island—her aunt had written.

By the way, Nikos has married Marika. Rumour is there's a baby on the way, but I guess no one worries about such things any more. You know, I always thought you and Nikos would marry, but I know King Giorgos would hate that. So you're best out of it.

Until then she'd hoped, desperately, that Nikos would follow her. But when she'd read that…

Marika was a distant relation of Nikos, giggly, flirtatious and ambitious. She'd always thought Marika was in love with her cousin, Demos— but obviously it had been Nikos all the time.

She'd been so shocked she'd been physically ill.

Then, four months later her aunt had written a much shorter note. *'A baby. A little girl for Nikos and Marika…'* Her note had trailed off, unfinished, and the writing on the envelope had been scrawly.

It was no wonder. The letter had been delivered two days after her aunt's death.

She'd wept then, for not going home in time, for not guessing her aunt was ill until she'd received the letter, for knowing her last link to the island was ended. And if she'd wept for the fact that Nikos had a baby with Marika, then so be it, the whole thing was grey.

'I'm sorry,' she said now, feeling useless. 'How…how long?'

'How long ago since she left? Nine years. It wasn't what you might call a long-term marriage.'

His tone was bitter. Oh, Nikos, she thought. You, too? Wounds might heal, but scars remained.

'I'm sorry,' she said again, but then made a belated attempt to pull herself together. 'But… it's nothing to do with me. Nothing from the island's anything to do with me. My aunt was the last family I had, and she's dead.'

'The whole island's your family. You rule.' It was said explosively, with passion, and Athena flinched and couldn't think how to reply.

The crêpes arrived, light and hot, oozing a wonderful lemon liqueur and doused with clotted cream. This was everything she most denied herself in food. Nikos picked up a fork and started in—then paused.

'What's wrong?'

'I didn't really want these.'

'You're ill?'

'No.'

'Then eat,' he said. 'You're stupidly thin.'

'I am not!'

'Are, too,' he said, and grinned and suddenly there it was again—the bossiness, the arguments, the *fun*. Childhood with Nikos had been wonderful. Magic.

'Can't make me,' she responded before she could help herself, a response she'd made over and over as a kid.

His dark eyes gleamed with challenge. 'Want to bet?'

'No!'

'Eat your crêpes, Thene.'

She smiled, despite herself, picked up a fork and ate.

How long since she'd indulged in something this full of calories? They tasted fantastic.

'You're not a model,' Nikos said, halfway through his crêpes and finally pausing for breath. 'Why starve?'

'It's expected,' she said. 'You can never be too rich or too thin.'

'Yeah, I've heard that, too,' he growled. 'So, they'll fire you if you gain a pound or six?'

'That party we were at tonight… If I'd turned

up as a size fourteen, you think I'd get a foot in the door?'

'You're invited to write about it. Not be it.'

'I'm part of the scene. They like their scene perfect.'

'And this is a career you like?'

'It beats pulling craypots.'

More silence. But he wasn't angry, she thought. He kept on eating, as if she'd just commented on the weather. She'd never been able to needle him.

Oh, she'd missed him. For ten long years it had felt like an ache, a limb missing, phantom pains shooting when she least expected. Watching him now, it felt as if she was suddenly whole again. He was intent on his pancake, maybe giving her space—who knew with Nikos?

He'd fitted right in with the people at the party, she thought. But then she thought, no. She'd got that wrong.

Nikos was an embodiment of what the people she worked with wanted to be. They went to gyms and solariums and plastic surgeons and every other expensive way to get their bodies to where Nikos had his.

All they had to do was haul fifty or so craypots a day for life, she thought, and found she was smiling.

'What?' he said, and she was suddenly smiling straight at him, almost pleading for him to return the smile.

And he did. In force. His smile had the capacity to knock her sideways.

The waiter, about to descend to take away their plates, paused with the strength of it. This was a classy establishment. Their waiter knew enough not to intrude on such a smile.

'I've missed you, Thene,' Nikos said, and his hand was reaching over the table for hers.

No. She found enough sense to tug her hands off the table and put them sensibly in her lap. But she couldn't stop herself saying the automatic reply. 'I've missed you, too.'

'So come home.'

'Because I've missed you?'

'Because the country needs you.'

Here it was again. Duty. Guilt.

'No.'

She closed her eyes and the waiter decided it was safe to come close. He cleared the plates and set them again, ready for soufflé. Maybe Nikos was watching her. She didn't know.

Duty.

It had torn her in two ten years ago. To go back now…

'You know Demos wants to open the diamond mines again?' he said, almost conversationally, and her eyes flew open.

'What the… Why?'

'He's wanted to for years. It was only Giorgos's greed that stopped him. Giorgos wasn't fussed about mining them—he had more money than he knew what to do with, thankfully. But the royal money chests have gone to Alexandros on Sappheiros. There's little money in the Argyros exchequer.'

'Which mines does he want to open?' She shouldn't care, she thought. She shouldn't!

'All of them.'

'*All?* The island will be ripped apart.'

'You think Demos cares?'

She stared at him, but she was no longer seeing him. Argyros… The Diamond Isles. Three magic island nations in the Mediterranean. All whitewashed stone, steep cliffs, sapphire seas. Three diamonds glittering in the sun.

Home.

Once upon a time the Isles had been three separate nations—Sappheiros, Argyros and Khryseis, but for the last two hundred years they'd been ruled as a Kingdom. Now, however, with the death of King Giorgos without an heir, the islands were Principalities again.

And she was Crown Princess Athena.

Ha. She'd walked away from the royal title when she'd walked away from the island, but it always had been a hollow tag.

Nikos had more right to rule than she, she thought. He'd lived and worked on Argyros all his life. He loved it.

And Demos?

Demos was the son of Athena's uncle. Because his father was younger than Athena's mother, he was second in the ancient lineage where she was first. But neither of them had expected to rule.

From time to time she'd read about Demos in the society pages. Whereas she'd left her title of

Princess on the island, Demos still valued the title Prince and he used it.

He'd phoned her a week ago and asked that she abdicate and leave the Crown to him. She'd tentatively agreed, because what was the alternative? Going home…going back herself was impossible.

'Demos arrived back on the island the day after we learned the King's rule was ended,' Nikos said, and she realised he'd been following her thoughts. 'He wants it so badly he'll do whatever it takes to get it. He's assuming you don't want it. Do you know why?'

'He rang and asked.'

'Alexandros rang you as well.'

'Yes.' Alexandros, the new crown Prince of Sappheiros, was trying to untangle the mess that was the succession.

'And you told him you were confused.'

'I was,' she said. 'Until Demos phoned.'

'So you'd let Demos have it?'

'It's an empty title anyway. Demos will enjoy it. And how can I come home now?' she demanded.

'It's not an empty title. Not if he opens the diamond mines.'

'It doesn't matter. It can't matter. My life is here.'

'It's not much of a life if it doesn't include crêpes. Or soufflé. Hey, look at this!'

The house speciality was arriving. The soufflé. This dish was famous. *How had Nikos manoeuvred his way in here?*

'Who do you think you are?' she demanded, and he grinned.

'A fisherman from Argyros. A kid in a lolly shop. Wow! Shut up and eat, Thene. This food needs serious respect.'

She opened her mouth to deny it. She so did not need another sweet.

Her raspberry soufflé was exploding upward and outward, crusty, dusted with sugar, irresistible. While she thought weakly about denial, the waiter produced a jug and poured a thin, hot trickle of blood-red juice down into the soufflé. The crust burst at the centre, the soufflé swallowed the juice and Athena conceded that maybe Nikos was right. This demanded serious respect.

She shut up and ate.

Heaven. Right here on the plate. Seriously wonderful food…

Missing out on such treats was the price she

paid for being where she was. If she got up at five tomorrow and jogged double her normal distance… Maybe…

'Let it go, Thene,' Nick said. He was wiping the inside of his bowl with his forefinger and licking in deep appreciation. 'You had a bigger butt when you were eleven. It's not natural.'

'It's what I do.' She finished and set down her spoon. Who licked their fingers?

She had a sudden blast of memory. Nikos's mother, Annia, standing at her kitchen table, endlessly baking. She remembered a plum pie that was to die for…

Before she could help herself, she let her finger drop into the bowl, ran it round the edges and licked. Not sure whether she was tasting soufflé now, or pie from the past.

'How's your mother?' she asked.

'Great,' Nikos said. 'She sends her love. She says come home—though if I take you home looking like this she'll have forty fits.'

'I loved your mother.'

It was said without thinking. She hadn't meant it. Or…she hadn't meant to say it.

'She hated it when you went away, Thene.'

'Yeah. Well.' Suddenly she'd had enough. More than enough. Emotion was threatening to overwhelm her. She stood up, too fast. It made her feel dizzy. Disoriented. Nikos was beside her in a flash, gripping her elbow, supporting her.

She should wrench away. He made her…melt.

'I need to go home.'

'My car's close.'

'You have a car? Here? In Manhattan?'

'Borrowed from Stefanos.'

Stefanos. Of course. The third member of the guardians.

Stefanos, Alexandros and Nikos had been friends from childhood. Three intelligent boys, bound by one common goal. To free their respective islands.

They'd run together as a pack. Only, of course, while Giorgos was alive they could do nothing. But now…

'Stefanos is still in New York?' she asked. She'd seen him once, when she'd walked into a city hospital to visit a friend. She'd turned and walked out before he'd seen her. She'd even thought of moving to another city because he was here. But that was ridiculous. It was a big city.

'Stefanos is in Australia trying to find the heir to the throne of Khryseis. He's Prince Regent of that island. Like you, he doesn't have a choice.'

'I do have a choice,' she snapped. 'And one of them is to make my own way home. To my home. To where I live now.'

'How do you get home from here?' he asked, as if mildly interested, not taking up her nuances. 'A cab? I'll drive you.'

'I ride the subway.'

'The subway…'

'This is my neighbourhood, Nikos,' she said, and made her voice sound sure and mature and…determined. 'This is where I live. But I need to go. Oscar and Nicholas are expecting me.'

'Who are Oscar and Nicholas?'

'My family,' she said, and the thought of Nicholas brought fear flooding back. 'So…so, if you'll excuse me… Oh, you need to pay? Sorry if I don't wait. Goodnight.'

And she turned and walked from the restaurant.

When she reached the pavement she slipped off her shoes and she started to run.

CHAPTER TWO

CARRIE was watching TV when she let herself into her apartment. Lovely, comforting Carrie, middle-aged and buxom, knitting endless squares to turn into endless blankets for the homeless. She closed the door, leant on it as if to lock the world out and let herself be comforted by the domesticity in front of her.

Oscar was lying draped over Carrie's feet. The big basset hound looked up at her with soulful reproach, as if to say, *You expect me to get up at this time of night? You need to be kidding.*

She smiled. Oscar helped as well.

'Hey, great jacket,' Carrie said equably from the couch. 'You swap jackets with a boy?'

Whoops. She'd forgotten she was wearing it. Or maybe subconsciously she'd known, and she liked it. She fingered the soft, worn leather and found comfort there as well.

'Yep,' she said.

'A good-looking one?'

'Yep to that as well. Really good-looking.'

'Excellent,' Carrie said and dumped her knitting into her carrier bag. 'He ask you out?'

'We did already. We ate soufflé and crêpes.'

'And crêpes? Wow. You going to see him again?'

'Once is enough.' Once in one lifetime.

Carrie's face puckered into disappointment. 'Why the heck?' she demanded, seriously displeased. 'You know I can take Nicky whenever you want. You need a love life.'

'I've had one.'

'But you've kept his jacket,' Carrie said, thoughtful. 'Smart girl. A guy's going to miss a jacket like that. Does he know where you live?'

'No. I'll post it to him.'

'Don't post it for a couple of days,' Carrie said. 'Give the man a challenge.' She pushed her more than ample self to her feet, made her way across the room and gave Athena a hug. 'You deserve some excitement. And Nicky needs a dad.'

'Carrie…'

'Just saying,' Carrie said placidly. 'Just going.' And she went. Leaving silence.

She sat, on cushions still warm from Carrie. She stared mindlessly at the soap Carrie had been watching. Oscar sighed, heaved himself sideways and redraped himself over her feet.

She needed comfort.

She needed to stop being angry.

Why the anger? After ten years, surely she had no right to still be angry with Nikos.

Or maybe she had. Ten years ago she'd ached for him to follow her. Just one word…something…a message to find out if she was okay. Her aunt had known her address. Nikos had known her aunt.

But it was as if the moment she'd walked off the island she'd walked out of Nikos's life. And now…here he was, demanding she take a part in the island's future. Demanding she think about Argyros.

And all she could think was that she hadn't told him he had a son.

He was here. The time to tell him was now.

The time to tell him was ten years ago. For him to find out now…

It had to happen. She had to find the courage.

Maybe he'd leave without trying to see her again. Maybe she'd have to go to Argyros to tell him.

He was in New York right now. She had to get over her anger and tell him.

And then say goodbye. For to go back to Argyros… Even if Demos were to destroy the island with his greed for diamonds…

No. It couldn't happen. She'd have to do something.

What?

Nothing, she told herself, but there was desperation behind the word.

It had to be nothing. She'd left Argyros behind. That first dreadful year, she'd coped with homesickness, isolation, fear, and the birth of Nicky, and she'd faced it alone. She'd fought to make herself a living, knowing she was all her baby had. *That which doesn't kill us makes us stronger.* The often used platitude had become her mantra.

She'd never again let herself need anyone as she'd needed Nikos. She no longer loved Nikos and she no longer called Argyros home.

Her head hurt. Thinking hurt.

She needed to sleep, but sleep wasn't going to come easily tonight. If she filed her story now… That'd mean tomorrow was free. Saturday—

Nicky had the day off school. They could go to the park…something, anything, just to get her away from here, buy her a little time.

She should take off Nikos's jacket.

Not yet. For just a little bit longer she'd allow herself that one small comfort.

Who the hell were Oscar and Nicholas?

Husband? Son? Sons? He was going nuts not knowing.

He'd hired someone to find her. The firm he'd hired had given him the magazine she worked for and a brief summary of her career. It was hardly personal.

Why had he never thought she could be married?

She wasn't wearing a ring.

That could mean anything. Rings weren't compulsory. Nor was marriage; its lack didn't necessarily mean you were without a long-term partner.

Why had she responded to him with anger?

He'd hardly expected her to fall into his arms as her long lost friend. He'd married someone else.

Marika… He thought of his ex-wife now and

fought back anger that stayed with him still. But you needed to move on. *He* needed to move on.

He had.

Or he thought he had until he'd seen Athena tonight. She was every bit the girl he remembered—but now she was a woman. Her eyes had tiny creases—smile lines. Did she smile often? Did the unknown Oscar and Nicholas make her smile?

He'd forgotten how she'd made him feel—or maybe he'd blocked it out. Looking at her across the restaurant table tonight…it had taken all the power he had to keep his voice neutral, to keep his feelings in check.

She was still Athena—the girl he'd loved to the point of madness—and then she'd chosen her career over him. The woman he'd held in a corner of his heart for ten long years.

Oh, there'd been other women—of course there had. As the owner of the biggest fishing fleet in the Diamond Isles he was considered more than eligible. He was never lost for…companionship, only every woman he dated compared with Athena.

Even the woman he'd married.

Especially the woman he'd married.

The old anger gripped him, tore at him. The old hunger…

Only it wasn't an old hunger. It was as real and as raw tonight as it had ever been.

He opened the door to the adjoining hotel room. The woman from the hotel sitting service rose to leave.

'She's been very good, sir. I read her the book like you said. She even undressed herself. I didn't think…'

'That's great,' he said. He didn't want to hear what she didn't think.

'Goodnight, then,' the woman said and slipped away into the night.

He stood for a moment gazing down at Christa. His daughter was sucking her thumb, even in sleep. She shouldn't—but who cared?

He crossed to the bed and sat down beside his sleeping child. He stroked her pretty dark hair. She opened her eyes and smiled sleepily at him. 'Papa.'

'Go to sleep, kitten,' he said softly.

'N…nice.' She closed her eyes again and was instantly asleep.

How could he still be angry? Athena had

moved away but now, in his heart, in her stead, he had his little daughter.

For years he'd tried to think that. It didn't work. It never had.

For years he'd envisaged Athena in a barren, lonely existence in a strange land. He'd almost hoped for it.

She'd left him. He should have cut off all thoughts of her. He shouldn't care.

But it wasn't possible. Not then and not now.

Athena…or his daughter.

Athena and the unknown Oscar and Nicholas.

So she had a family, too. Well, so be it, he thought, trying to be rational. He had his Christa and he was content. What he was feeling now was the echoes of the past. From now on the personal had to be set aside for the good of the island.

Tomorrow he had to find her again. She had to face her duty. She must.

He'd take Christa sightseeing tomorrow morning. Maybe they could take a buggy ride round Central Park. She'd enjoy that. Then, in the afternoon, he'd go to see Athena again.

And get his jacket back.

He thought of his jacket as he'd last seen it, draped round Athena's shoulders as she'd fled the restaurant. Maybe he should have followed her.

But…and it was a big but. There had been fear in her eyes as she'd fled. Real fear.

He didn't know why. He intended to find out, but for now… He was inexplicably glad she'd worn his jacket home.

How could she explain a man's jacket to the unknown Nicholas and Oscar? Unaccountably, he found himself smiling. He hoped they were good to her. Yeah, that was a rational thought. Generous, even.

But…she had to come back to the island, even if it meant she brought this unknown Oscar and Nicholas with her. Though their existence could make things much more complicated.

Whatever. Tomorrow could be faced tomorrow, he told himself, trying to block out the unwanted image of Athena with another man by her side. Trying to block out how it made him feel. After all this time, surely jealousy was crazy.

Of course it was.

He kissed his daughter softly on the forehead, the touch and scent of her soft little body helping him put things into perspective.

'Goodnight, sweetheart,' he whispered. 'We'll have a good time tomorrow; just see if we don't. And then we'll persuade the Princess Athena to come home. Where we belong and where she belongs, too.'

In the morning the sun finally decided to shine. Nikos and his little daughter did the circuit of Central Park twice, and then they did it again. Christa's unalloyed happiness, the sun on her face, the beauty of the horses, the garishness of the decoration on the buggy…she loved it. She clung to him, breathless with excitement, laughing out loud for sheer joy.

Halfway through their third circuit he saw Athena.

And a dog.

And a child.

How could it be? How could fate be this cruel?

Why on earth had she decided to come to a tourist destination this morning?

Stupid, stupid, stupid.

They'd been using their ball-thrower. Dogs were supposed to be on leads here, but she knew a place…most dog owners did. So they'd tossed the ball until Oscar was out of puff. Nicky had run more than the dog. Oscar wasn't the brightest light on the Christmas tree, so about half the time it had been Nicky who'd had to retrieve it. Finally they'd bought ice cream cones and now they were waiting for Oscar to finish his before they walked home.

Oscar, a big, lumbering bear of canine dopiness, took his ice cream eating seriously.

A horse and buggy was wheeling briskly along the path towards them. The horses looked gorgeous, she thought. The day was gorgeous, making up for last night's misery. She was dumb to be anxious on a day like this.

She chuckled at Oscar's pink nose.

The buggy grew closer. The driver raised his crop in salute. It was that sort of day.

She smiled. She waved back.

And then she saw who was in the buggy.

Nikos.

And a child?

The sounds around them faded. Everything faded.

She heard Nikos's snapped order as if it came from a distance. The buggy stopped. Nikos climbed down, paid the driver and lifted the little girl down after him.

The child was little and dark and beautifully dressed, in a pink dress with a wide pink bow, white socks edged with pink lace and shiny pink shoes. A pink Alice band held back her glossy black hair. Shoulder-length with bangs.

Smiling and smiling.

Down's syndrome.

The little girl laughed as Nikos swung her down, and Nikos laughed back.

Athena's heart did a back flip. Landed upside down, somewhere else in her chest than where it should be.

Down's syndrome…

Her aunt's letter came back to her.

'A little girl for Nikos and Marika…'

'Hi,' she managed, and if her voice came out a squeak she couldn't help it.

'Hi,' Nikos said back. He sounded as incredulous as she was—and as wary. The horse and buggy bowled on, leaving Nikos and his daughter on the verge of the path.

Nikos wasn't looking at her. He was looking at Nicky.

Nicky, who was the spitting image of his father—a mirror image of the younger Nikos.

Father…and son.

She should have…she should have…

It was too late for should haves. The time was now.

'This is Christa,' Nikos said at last, and his voice seemed to come from a distance. 'Christa, this is my friend, Athena.'

'Dog,' Christa said in Greek, still smiling. Pointing to Oscar. 'Ice… Ice cream.'

The ice cream vendor was right behind them. 'Would…would you like an ice cream, Christa?' Athena asked, and then thought desperately, what if she had a dairy allergy. What if…

'Yes,' Christa said, very firmly. She looked up at her father, searched for another word and found it. 'Please.'

She smiled again. She was gorgeous, Athena thought, and suddenly found she was blinking back tears. Nikos was holding his little daughter's hand with pride. With tenderness. With love.

'Ice cream, Papa?' Christa asked and Nikos nodded. He hadn't taken his eyes from Nicky.

'Introduce us,' he said.

'This is Nicky,' she said, trying to find the right words. And then, because she didn't want him to get the wrong idea—even if there was no denying the wrong idea was right—she added quickly, 'Nicholas.'

'Of course,' he said. Non-committal. 'And the dog?'

'Oscar.' She turned away—fast. 'I'll buy Christa a cone. Would you like one?'

'No. Thank you.'

It took time to get the cone. There were people queuing ahead of her. Then she thought she should have asked Christa what she wanted. But somehow…she knew. Strawberry.

And she was right. 'Pink,' Christa said with huge pleasure. She looked at the bench where Nicky and Oscar were seated. 'Sit,' she said.

Nicky smiled and shifted, just slightly, so there was room for Christa to sit between him and Oscar.

Athena thought, I'm going to cry.

She was *not* going to cry.

Still Nikos said nothing. Neither did she.

Words were too big. Or too small. There was nothing to fill this silence.

Finally Nikos found words that might do. For now. Filler words. 'It's good to meet you, Nicholas. Is Oscar your dog or your mother's?'

'Mine,' Nicky said and she thought, great question. Generally shy, discussions of Oscar made Nicky blossom.

'How old is he?'

'We're not sure. He was in our street one day when we came home. He was dirty and really, really hungry. We took him to the animal shelter 'cos Mama said someone might be looking for him, but no one wanted him so we got him back. I called him Oscar 'cos Mama told me she had a dog called Oscar when she was little. Before my Mama's mama died.'

'I remember Oscar,' Nikos said softly, gravely. 'He was great. If your Oscar's like him he must be really special.'

'He is.'

'Does he eat everything like that?' Oscar was still licking, stretching the experience for as long as he could. Nicky had chosen a rainbow ice cream for him and he'd wedged it between the planks on the bench. Oscar had a paw on either side of the cone so it couldn't tip. His nose colour had changed now to green.

'He enjoys his pleasures, does Oscar,' Athena said, and Nikos finally looked at her. Really looked at her.

The look would stay with her all her life, she thought numbly. Disbelief. Awe. Anger. And raw, undisguised pain.

'He is, isn't he?' he asked, and there was only one way to answer that.

'He is.'

He closed his eyes.

Where to go from here?

'You can't do this, Thena,' he said, and his voice was suddenly harsh. 'No more. You walked away with *this*…'

'I didn't know.' It was a cry of pain but she knew it was no excuse.

'You walked away. And now…' He paused, took a deep breath, then another. 'Leave it,' he said and she wasn't sure if he was talking to himself or to her. 'I can't take it in. Just come back to the island and we'll sort it there. We need to get the succession in place. If you don't come home the island will be ruined. How selfish can you be?'

'Selfish?' She would have gasped if she hadn't felt so winded. 'Me? Selfish.' Then, before she could stop herself she produced the question that had slammed at her heart for almost ten years. 'How old is Christa?'

'Nine.'

'And her birthday is when?'

'June.'

'So there you go,' she snapped, the old, stupid grief welling up in her all over again. 'Nicky's nine and he was born in September. What does that tell you, Nikos?'

'Nothing,' he snapped. 'Except that you should have told me.'

'So maybe you should have asked. When I left…there was nothing.'

'You told me not to follow.'

'I didn't expect you to believe me,' she yelled—really yelled—and everyone looked at her. Even Oscar. Christa's ice cream started to drip on the side she wasn't licking. Nikos automatically stooped and turned it around for her, wiping her chin before it dripped on her dress.

It was a tiny gesture but, for some stupid reason, the sight of it cut through her anger and made her want to weep again.

'It's time we went home,' she whispered, and Nicky looked up at her in surprise.

'We were going to walk right round.'

'I'm tired.'

'I'm not,' he said, clearly astonished.

'Tell you what,' Nikos said. 'Why don't we compromise. Nicky, I'm from the island where your mother was born. I know your mama just shouted at me, but maybe that's because…because we both got a shock. Your mother and I have known each other since we were children, but this is the first time I've been to New York.'

'Yes…' Nicky said, not sure where this conversation was going.

'What if Christa stays here with your mama? Christa gets tired easily—she has a problem with her heart that makes her tired. But she'll be happy here with a dog and an ice cream. So your mama and Christa can rest here. Christa can finish her ice cream and you can show me all the way round.'

Nicky looked doubtfully at his mother. She was too numb to respond.

'Thene,' Nikos said urgently, and she tried to pull herself together. What was he asking? Fine, she decided. Anything. The gods would have to take control from now on. She couldn't.

'Can I take Oscar?' Nicky asked.

'Yes,' Nikos said.

'You really knew my mother when she was little?' her son asked.

'When she was Princess Athena,' Nikos told him. 'Your mother needs to be Princess Athena again. Come with me and I'll tell you why. Will Oscar come with us?'

Nicky was looking at her. Waiting for her approval.

What did it matter? She was no longer in control here. She knew nothing.

'Fine,' she said weakly. 'Take…take your time. Christa and I will look at the zoo.'

She sat on the bench and watched Christa finish her ice cream, and the desire to weep grew almost overwhelming.

What was it with men? How could she have thrown those two birth dates together and have Nikos react without the slightest regret? Or shame. Or guilt.

He'd called her selfish for leaving the island. She'd told him she wanted to leave for an exciting job in New York and he'd looked at her with shock and disbelief—and he'd let her walk away.

But if he knew the true reason… That if she'd stayed his family would be ruined. That the old King had threatened everything Nikos loved if she stayed. How could he never have guessed?

He'd never, ever asked. He'd never so much as written. And, when she'd learned of Christa's birth, she knew the reason why he hadn't.

Her fingers were clenched into her palms so hard they hurt.

'Papa,' Christa said suddenly, as if she'd just realised Nikos was gone. She looked worried.

This wasn't Christa's fault. She had no right to let her own misery and confusion spread to this little girl. 'He'll be back soon,' she said gently.

'Papa.'

'There's a little zoo just near here. Do you like animals?'

The little girl considered. 'Big?' she asked.

'Little. Funny animals. Friends.'

'Friends,' Christa said and put out a hand for Athena to help her to her feet. She smoothed her dress, tucked a sticky hand into Athena's and had another lick of her ice cream. 'Friends.'

There were so many questions… Where to start? An inquisition could be a good way to send Nicky straight back to his mother.

'Where do you go to school?' he asked, and then thought, great, very insightful. Not.

'Over there,' the little boy told him, pointing south east.

Good. That got him places. 'Do you like school?'

'Sometimes. I hafta go to Greek lessons after school, too.'

'You speak Greek?'

'Mama does. She makes me.'

He needed time to take that one in.

They walked along. Kicking stones. Nikos suddenly realised… He was kicking stones in front of him. So was Nicky. With his left foot.

'You're left-handed?'

'Mmm,' Nicky said.

'Your mama's right-handed.'

'Mmm.'

Riveting stuff. Both being left-handed. It meant nothing.

It meant everything.

'Has your mother told you about Argyros?'

'Yes,' he said. 'Are you a fisherman?'

'Yes.'

'I like boats.'

'Have you been on boats?'

'Twice. I don't get seasick. Mama does. This is the place where a Beatle was shot.'

'Right,' Nikos said. He gave up. There were too many questions for one small boy to handle.

There were too many questions for him to handle.

They were sitting right where he'd left them, only Christa had replaced her ice cream with a hand puppet. A squirrel.

She wiggled it as they approached, her face lighting up as she saw him.

'Thena bought…me…squirrel.' He grinned and swung her up into his arms. No matter what else was happening here, this mustn't touch her. That had been his mantra for almost ten years and he wasn't budging now.

'Thank you,' he said gravely to Athena.

'We didn't get all the way round,' Nicky said. 'We caught another buggy. Nikos says John was his favourite Beatle. He was yours too, wasn't he, Mama?'

'Yes,' she said, sounding repressive.

'Imagine,' he said softly and watched her wince.

It had been the last night they'd been together. 'I have to go away,' she'd said, but she'd sobbed and clung.

He hadn't understood why she had to leave. She'd completed her university degree by correspondence, far younger than most. Her writing was brilliant. Everyone said so. She could take a job with the local paper and write the novel to end all novels. They'd agreed. She could stand by him in his battle with Giorgos.

That was what they'd planned, but suddenly she was crumpled, broken, sobbing about having to leave.

'I need to go. I just need to go. Please, Nikos, don't make it any harder.'

He'd thought it was her writing that was driving her. 'You'll come back?'

'I don't know. I can't. Nikos…'

She'd run out of words. He'd been angry, shocked, bewildered.

That night in his family's boatshed… Their last night. He'd played music by John Lennon on his tinny little sound system.

Imagine…

He thought now: Nicky must have been conceived that night.

No matter. He had to get rid of the white noise. There was only one absolute. 'You need to come home,' he told her.

'No.'

'Then Demos wins.' He made an almost superhuman effort to rid himself of his emotional tangle and concentrate on what was important. 'I need to go home tomorrow,' he said. 'I thought I had a week to persuade you, but Demos has already contacted mining companies. He's acting as if he owns the place. I daren't stay longer. But it's your birthright, Athena. And,' he added, 'it's your son's.'

'And your…'

'And my daughter's,' he finished for her, harshly. For maybe she was going places he wasn't ready to go just yet. 'Our children's. You must come home.'

'No.'

'Think about it,' he said briefly, harshly. 'There's so much happening here I can't take it in. Whatever's gone on in the past…' He glanced at Nicky and felt as if he was on a shifting deck, unsure of his footing, unsure of anything. 'For now we need to put that aside. If you don't come home, then some time soon I'll be back here to…sort what's mine. But my priority right now has to be the islanders. Thousands of livelihoods, Thena. Princess Athena. They're your people. You answer to them and not to me. Except…'

He hesitated and then said the words that had to be said. The words that had been in his head for the entire tour of the park.

'Except on the question of my son,' he said.

She gasped. 'That's not fair.'

'Life's not fair. Get over it, Athena, and come home. Princess.'

Nicky had been listening on the sidelines, troubled, not understanding but trying. 'You said *my son*,' he pointed out, trying to be helpful. 'Did you mean your daughter?'

Nikos nodded. Grave as Nicky. 'I must have,' he agreed. 'But I'm a bit upset right now. I need your mama to come back to the island where she was born.'

'You called her a princess.'

'She is a princess.'

'She's my Mama.'

'She can be both. I bet your mama says you can be anything you want if you try hard enough.' He turned and faced Athena straight on. She was lovely, he thought. In her casual sweatshirt, her jeans, her tumbled curls tied back with a piece of red ribbon… She was a mature version of the girl he'd fallen for ten years ago. Longer. The girl he'd loved for ever.

He couldn't think that.

'Your mama can do anything she wants,' he said to Nicky, but he kept right on looking at Athena. 'I think it's time for your mama to do just that. Because I think she wants the island of Argyros to be safe just as much as I do.'

CHAPTER THREE

So two weeks later… Maybe she was out of her mind, but she was going back to a place she'd thought she'd never set foot on again. Argyros. The Silver Island of the Diamond Isles.

If Giorgos had had a son this never would have happened.

Generations of islanders had ached for the islands to revert to the three principalities they had once been. Now with Giorgos's death, they had.

'But why did it have to happen on my watch?' Athena muttered as she stood on the deck of the Athens-Argyros ferry and watched her island home grow bigger.

Beside her was Nicky. He was practically bursting with excitement. He should be in school, she thought. How could he get into the college of his choice if she kept interrupting his education?

That was only one of the arguments she'd thrown at Nikos during the tense phone calls that followed his visit. But always it had returned to the bottom line.

If she backed away from her role as Crown Princess then Demos would open all six diamond mines.

Whereas Nikos had a very different proposal—to open one mine, avoiding mess and with minimal effect on the island's environment. Profits to go into the island's infrastructure and the island could prosper.

Nikos had told her all of this by phone, talking of nothing but the island, making no mention of how these children had happened, how Nicky and Christa affected their future—nothing, nothing, nothing.

Apart from that one outburst in the park, he'd contained his rage.

As she'd contained hers. We've been civilised, she thought, and tried to feel proud of herself.

Instead she felt small. Belittled by the latent anger she heard behind Nikos's civility. Frightened of what lay ahead.

'How long will we stay?' By her side at the

rails, Nicky suddenly sounded as scared as she was. 'For ever?'

'I've taken a month's leave. I'm hoping by the end of the month Nikos should be able to take over the running of the place.'

'Running?'

'Like…the government. If I can organise things then Nikos will be the government when I leave.'

'Are you the government now?'

'Technically, yes. Though my cousin has been filling in.'

'We don't like your cousin Demos?'

'I'm not sure we do,' she said. 'Nikos says he's greedy. But let's just see for ourselves, shall we?'

'Okay,' he said and tucked his hand into hers, with the infinite trust of childhood.

She needed someone to trust too, she thought. What was she letting herself in for?

'We'll just slip in quietly, do what we have to do and leave,' she said. 'I'm hoping we'll hardly be noticed. I'll show you the places where I swam and played when I was a little girl. I'll figure how to stop Demos digging his great big diamond mines. Then we can go home, with as little contact with the locals as possible.'

'So we won't see Nikos and Christa?' He sounded astounded. More. Sad.

'I guess we will,' she said and he lit up again.

'Good. I like them. Christa likes Oscar.'

'Oscar.' She glanced down at the dog on the deck beside her. Crazy. Coming all this way and bringing a dog.

But she needed to. She needed as much family as she could get. Nicky and Oscar were it.

We slip in quietly, do what we need to do and leave, she said to herself again, as she'd told herself countless times before. I'll give Nikos the authority he needs and leave.

But what about…Nicky? The small matter of Nikos's son.

It can't matter, she thought. Yes, Nikos was angry—maybe he even had a right to that anger, but there was still the matter of Christa, conceived three months before Nicky. When he and she…

It didn't bear thinking about.

'We'll get in, do what we have to and get out again,' she said again to Nicky. 'No fuss. Nothing.'

And then the boat passed the headland and

turned towards the harbour. And she discovered that no fuss wasn't in the island's equation.

She'd come. Right up until now he'd thought she'd back out. But he knew she'd boarded the ferry in Athens. Short of jumping off, she had to be here.

So he'd let it be known. Demos had been acting Crown Prince. If Athena arrived on the quiet, as if she didn't want the Crown, it would give everyone the wrong idea. The islanders were terrified by Demos's plans. They needed Athena.

And…they knew her.

The only child of a lone and timid mother, home schooled because the King didn't want her to mix with the island children, Athena had every reason to be isolated and aloof. But Athena had been irrepressible. Born a tomboy, she'd declared, aged eight, that Nikos was her very best friend and whatever he did was cool with her.

As children they'd roamed the island, looking for mischief, looking for adventure, looking for fun. Tumbling in and out of trouble. Giving their respective mothers cause for palpitations.

He'd loved her. The islanders had loved her.

They had been kids, who together just might make a difference to this island's future.

And now that time had come. He watched the ferry dock and knew that how Athena reacted in the next few moments affected the future of every islander.

Including him.

'Mama, why are all these people here?'

'Uh-oh,' she said.

'What does *uh-oh* mean?'

'It means Nikos is making a statement.'

'What sort of statement?'

'That I'm a princess coming home,' she said.

'So the streamers and balloons and the great big signs…'

'Saying Welcome Home To Our Princess? That would be for us.'

'What do we do?'

'I'm not sure. Stay on board until they get tired of waiting and go home?'

'I don't think that's a good idea,' Nicky said dubiously.

So it wasn't a good idea, she conceded. It was an excellent idea. But she knew Nikos was down there. She knew how much he loved this island and she knew for certain that if she didn't walk back onto her island home he'd come aboard and carry her.

Balloons had drifted into the water. A couple of excited kids had jumped in to retrieve them, and the ferry captain was forced to reverse and wait for his men to verify it was safe to dock.

Nikos watched and waited, feeling as if he shouldn't be here. Feeling as if he had no choice.

The islanders were going crazy. Their pleasure in Athena's arrival was a measure of how terrified they'd been that Demos would destroy them. It was also a measure of confidence that Athena wouldn't betray them.

Did he believe it?

Up until she was nineteen he'd believed it. He and Athena had plotted what they'd do if Giorgos was to die without an heir.

He grinned now as he thought of their plans. They'd build a cinema. They'd set up a surf school—Thena thought she'd make a great surf instructor—and what the heck, they'd invite a few rock groups over. But in their serious moments they'd had a few more solemn ideas. They'd slow-start the diamond mines. They'd ensure every child had the funds to get a decent education. They'd set up a democracy.

All of these things had been discussed over and over, as they'd wandered the island, as she'd come with him in his family's fishing boat and helped him haul pots, as she'd sat at his mother's kitchen table and helped shell peas or stir cakes.

When had he first figured he loved her? It had crept up on him so slowly he hardly knew. But suddenly their laughter had turned to passion, and their intensity for politics had turned to intensity of another kind.

The night her mother had died… She'd been seventeen. He'd cradled her against his heart and thought his own heart would break.

And then…suddenly it had been over. It seemed she had a chance of a journalist apprenticeship in New York.

Leaving had never been in his vocabulary, and he'd never believed it could be in hers.

And now she'd returned—she was standing at the ferry's rail looking lost, and he was standing on the jetty wondering where he could take it from here.

She had Nicky by the hand. Mother and son. And dog. The sight made him feel… Hell, he didn't know how he felt.

'Go on, Nikos.' His mother, Annia, was beside him, holding Christa. 'Go and speak for all the islanders. You know it's your place.'

'It's not my place.'

'It is,' Annia said fiercely. 'No one else will do it.'

And hadn't that always been the case?

As the King's sister, Nikos's mother had always stood up to the old King. She'd fought for the islanders' rights and, as he'd matured, Nikos had taken her fights onto his own shoulders.

He'd built up a fishing fleet that was second to none, but the islanders knew he worked for the whole island. They looked to him now as leader. He was in an uncomfortable position but he had no choice—there was no one else willing or able to take it on.

And now… If the only way Athena would rule was for him to stand beside her and guide her every step of the way, then he'd do it. He'd been raised to love this island, and he would not see it destroyed.

So now… He shoved aside anger, loss, confusion, a host of mixed emotions he wasn't near to understanding, and he strode up the gangplank with the determination of a man who knew where his duty lay. And, as he reached Athena, he took her in his arms and he hugged her. Whether she willed it or not. Whether he willed it or not.

'Welcome home,' he said and lifted her and swung her round in his arms, a precarious thing to do on a gangplank, but jubilation was called for. 'Princess Athena, welcome,' he said in a voice to be heard by all. 'We all welcome you, don't we?' he demanded of the crowd, and the islanders roared their assent.

'It's our royal family,' someone yelled. 'Princess Athena and Prince Nikos.'

'Nikos is only a prince if he marries Athena,' someone else yelled and there was a huge cheer of enthusiasm.

'Hey, Demos is already a prince. Maybe she should marry him,' someone yelled as the applause died, and the crowd laughed. The laughter was derisive.

And Nikos glanced to the back of the crowd and saw Demos. Even from this distance his body language was unmistakable. He was rigid with mortification and with fury.

Athena had a real enemy there, he thought. In the mood he was in, Demos could do harm.

Not if he stayed close.

He had no choice. In order to protect this island then he needed to protect this woman. He intended to stay very close indeed.

Athena's smile looked pinned in place. She was terrified, he thought.

'It's okay,' he murmured.

'No,' she murmured back. 'It's not okay at all. I'm doing this because I have no choice. If you think I like being hugged by you…'

The crowd's cheers were building. Athena waved and so did Nicky.

And Nikos had no choice either. He waved.

They stood together.

'There's a reception tonight at the palace,' he told her.

'There's a what?'

They were all in the royal limousine, heading

for the palace. Nikos hadn't wanted to come with her, but once again there'd been no choice. Someone had to introduce her to the palace staff.

He'd brought Christa along, to lighten the atmosphere a bit. To stop things getting too personal. Oscar lay on the floor looking exhausted. It had been a very long waddle down the gangplank.

Giorgos would have had a fit if he could have seen this dog in his limo, Nikos thought and suppressed a grin.

The limousine, the palace, these trappings of royalty, had been kept so Giorgos could come in state whenever he wished. They could get rid of it all now, Nikos thought, but then he considered the crowd who'd turned up to see Athena arrive. They'd cheered her with joy. She was giving the island its identity back. Did she even realise it?

'A reception,' he repeated, trying to get his head round practicalities. 'Everyone who's anyone on the island and a few more. Three hundred people.'

'How many?'

'You need to make a statement.'

'I don't.'

'Of course you do,' he said flatly. 'That's what you've come for.'

'But I'm not staying,' she said, sounding desperate. 'Nikos, I can't do this. A reception. People cheering. It's not who I am.'

'It's what you were born to.'

'I was born to be nothing.'

'That's a dumb statement.'

'Do you need to sound angry?'

'I'm not…'

'What have I done to make you angry, Nikos?' she demanded, suddenly as angry as he was.

'I could tell you.' He glanced across at Nicky. 'But not here.'

'Why not?'

'It's hardly…appropriate.'

'How about if I decide that?' she snapped.

They were being chauffeured along the magnificent coastal road that wound round headland after headland, stretching on until it reached the Royal Palace of Argyros. But Athena wasn't looking at scenery. She was focused on him.

'I don't think…'

'How about we stop thinking?' she snapped.

She closed her eyes for a long moment. Then she opened them and she reached for her son's hand.

Nicky had been alternately looking out of the window and looking at his mother. He was a smart kid, Nikos thought. He could hear the undercurrents of her anger. There were things going on that he didn't understand and he obviously didn't like it.

'Nicky, I want you to listen for a bit,' Athena said. 'Full attention.'

He gave it.

Athena glanced at Nikos. Glanced away. Took a deep breath.

'Nicky, when I saw the people at the boat,' she said, faltering for a start and then making her voice firmer. 'I realised there was something that Nikos and I need to tell you. That maybe we should have told you before this. Do you remember asking about who your father is? I told you your father was someone I met when I was very young. I told you that he was my best friend, but then he married someone else. That man is Nikos, Nicky. Nikos is your papa.'

What the…? What had she just said?

She'd taken all the wind out of his sails and then some.

It had clearly astounded Nicholas as well. 'Nikos is… Nikos is…' Nicky said and faltered to a stop, staring at him as if he had two heads.

'Do you see his hair?' All at once Athena sounded weary—strained to breaking point. 'It's the same colour as yours. It curls the same. You see how that little bit sticks up right at the top of Nikos's head? Yours does, too.'

Nicky stuck his hand on top of his head and felt the offending tuft. His eyes grew enormous.

It was all Nikos could do not to do the same.

'I told you that your papa was a fisherman,' Athena said. 'That's what Nikos is. Isn't that right, Nikos?'

She'd given him a son. Just like that. Like it or not.

Where to go from here?

She should have done this nine years ago, he thought, dazed, fighting anger, but knowing instinctively that his anger was no reason to mess with things now. To say no, let's talk about this at a more sensible time. Maybe we need DNA tests. Maybe we need…counselling. Or something?

Nicky was looking at him with eyes that were blank with shock. What happened in the next few moments would affect him for ever. He didn't need a counsellor to tell him that.

He had the power to mess this for life.

So where to go? What to say when you've just been given the gift of a son?

'I should have been there for your mother,' he said softly. 'I should have been around for you. I'm very, very sorry that I wasn't.'

'Why weren't you?' Nicky said.

And there was only one answer. Only the truth would serve.

'I didn't know,' he said heavily. 'Your mother left the island a long time ago, when she was expecting you. And she didn't tell me you were born. Maybe because we were both very young she thought it was the right thing to do. Maybe she thought it would be easier to bring you up on her own when I lived so far away. I wish I'd known, Nicky, but that's in the past. What's important now is that you're my son. I'm so proud that your mother's finally told me about you. I'm so proud to finally have the chance to know you.'

He glanced at Athena and her eyes were

brimful of tears. She wrenched her head around so she was looking out of the window, but not before he'd seen those tears.

'I'd like to teach you to fish,' he told Nicky, fighting for something—anything—to say. Hell, there should be a book on what he was doing now. It was too important to mess with, and all he could do was flounder. 'I'd love to take you in my boat.'

'You really own a fishing boat?'

'Really.'

'I don't get seasick,' Nicky said, as if that was important.

'Neither do I,' Nikos said and felt something grow in his chest. *The heart swells to fit all comers.* Maybe the corny saying was right.

His son. The thought was overwhelming.

Nicky and Christa. His son and his daughter.

His family.

'You have a grandma,' he said.

'A grandma.' Nicky was clearly overwhelmed.

'Her name is Annia. She's a princess like your mother.'

'My grandmother's a princess?'

'She's not as pretty a princess as your mother,'

Nikos told him. 'And, like your mother, she doesn't wear a tiara. But I hope you'll like… I hope you'll love her. She's a better fisherman than I am.'

'Does she get seasick?'

'No one in my family gets seasick,' he said and he saw Athena flinch.

Nicky fell silent. No one spoke. Athena was looking out of the window as if her life depended on it.

'Why didn't you tell me, Mama?' Nicky asked and the question hung. For a moment he thought she wasn't going to answer. For a moment he thought, how could she?

'I was very young,' she said at last, and her voice sounded as if it came from a long way away. 'I was in America and I was by myself. And I knew…I knew Nikos…your papa…and his wife were having a baby here. That baby is Christa. So I thought your papa needed to stay here to take care of Christa. I knew I could take care of you, and I did.'

And behind those words? Raw, unresolved pain. Bleak. Stark. Dreadful.

How to take that pain away?

Nikos knew that he couldn't. Ten years of pain, and the only way he could alleviate it was a truth that wasn't his to tell.

And he hadn't caused that pain. It was Athena who'd left.

'Why didn't you come back here?' Nicky asked her, obviously fighting to find some sense in all this.

'I have a great job, Nicky,' Athena said. 'I needed to work to support you.'

'But…' Nicky paused and looked from Athena to Nikos and back again. His mother and his father, and a history he didn't understand.

This was too heavy, Nikos thought. It was way, way too hard. Maybe they should have left this for the future, for some more appropriate time to tell him, but what was done was done. And somewhere in this mess they had to find joy.

He had a son. Yes, there was heartache and regret but he had a son, and his son needed to lose that look of confusion and…and yes, even the echo of his own sense of betrayal.

'See that rock out there in the bay?' he said, fighting for the right note. 'The big one with the flat top about two hundred yards from shore?'

'Mmm,' Nicky said, still dazed.

'I taught your mother to dive off that rock. Or I tried to. She kept doing bellywhackers.'

'I did not,' Athena retorted, struggling not to falter, and he knew that where he went she'd follow. How could she help it now?

'You did, too,' he said, and managed a strained sort of grin. 'You get your mama to take you out and show you her diving skills,' he told Nicky. 'She'll do bellywhackers every single time.'

'Christa, can you swim?' Athena asked, still sounding desperate, and Nikos thought maybe he'd got it right. He'd deflected the father bit, giving Nicky time to come to terms with it as he wanted.

He knew there was a lot more discussion to come. Some of that would have to be personal, between Athena and Nicky.

Some of that needed to be between himself and Athena.

'I like…swimming,' Christa said. She'd pushed her shoes off—she hated shoes—and her feet were resting on Oscar. 'I like…dog.'

'I think Oscar likes you,' Athena said.

'Does this mean Christa is my sister?' Nicky

asked and Nikos's thoughts went flying again. The issues were too big. Huge.

'I guess she is,' Athena said softly. 'Your half-sister.' Then she said gently, 'Christa has something called Down's syndrome. That means she was born with something a little different from most children. All the bits that start a baby growing…they're called chromosomes. Christa got an extra one. It makes the tips of her ears a bit small. It makes her tongue a little bit big and her eyes really dark and pretty. And it affects her in other ways too, including her speech.'

'But she likes Oscar.'

'She does,' Athena said gravely, smiling at Christa. 'I think Christa is our friend already. I think having her as your sister might be really cool.'

So much for leading the conversation, Nikos thought. It was now about the three of them. He was right out of the equation.

Somewhere, once, he'd read some scathing comment on fatherhood. Mothers knew all about their children's dramas, their love lives, the spots on the back of their necks. Fathers were vaguely aware there were short people in the house.

Not him, he thought. With Christa, he'd been so much more hands on. But he felt sidelined here.

'I wanted a sister,' Nicky was saying, cautious. 'A little sister. But Christa's nine.'

'I'm nine,' Christa said, nodding grave agreement.

'But she's much shorter than you,' Thena said. 'I think she always will be, so that means she'll always be your little sister.'

'So I get to look after her?'

'If you want.'

'Do I hafta share?'

'I guess you and Christa can work those things out for yourselves,' Athena said, and Christa looked at Nicky and beamed.

'Nicky,' she said.

'Brother,' Nicky said importantly and thumped his chest.

'Brother,' Christa repeated and thumped her chest.

They giggled.

Just like that, Nikos thought, stunned. It was over, just like that. Yeah, there'd be complications. Yeah, there'd be difficulties. But, for now…it was sorted.

'Now,' Athena said in a voice that boded ill.

'Now?'

'What about this reception?'

What were they thinking? Talking of social events when she'd casually given him his son? He felt as if all the wind had been sucked from his lungs and he wasn't the least sure how to get it back.

Nicky and Christa were looking at each other, sizing each other up, still grinning. Occasionally giggling. Having a sister was obviously a big deal for Nicky. Bigger than having a father?

He'd missed out on nine years of having a son. He looked back to Athena and she was looking as dazed as he was.

'I wanted to tell you,' she whispered. 'I didn't know how.'

'Like...the phone?' He couldn't keep anger from his voice and he got anger in return.

'You think? So I should have phoned you—and your wife—and thought about the consequences later?'

A host of angry rejoinders crowded his head. None of them could be said in front of the children.

Maybe none could be said at all.

'The reception,' she said again flatly, moving on.

'Seven tonight.' That, at least, was easy. 'The Crown Prince and Princess of Sappheiros will be welcoming home the Crown Princess of Argyros. Officially handing over control.'

'And then what?' He saw panic flare. 'Nikos, I can't do this alone. I can't do this at all. Run this country? I have no experience. I have nothing to qualify me for such a role. I've taken four weeks' leave. That's it.'

'If that's it, then you're handing the Crown to Demos.'

'This isn't fair.'

'Life's not,' he said shortly. He had evidence of this right in front of him. He'd had a son for nine years and he hadn't known.

She stared at him, speechless. He stared out of the window. Tried not to think that yes, it was unfair. As kids they'd planned to do this side by side. They still could if she…if he…

It had to be thought of. The lawyers had demanded he think of it.

How could he think about it?

'You *will* be there tonight,' she said urgently,

and a blunt voice inside him said no, let her sink. Not telling him he had a son…

But then he looked at her, he caught the terror, and he caught something else.

The Athena he'd once loved. She was still in there.

And this island… It was his home and he loved it. He had to support her, come what may.

And he had to convince her to stay.

Enough. One step at a time.

'I'll be there,' he told her.

'With me,' she said urgently. 'I won't remember names. People will know me and I won't remember them. I'll say the wrong thing. Nikos, you have to help me.'

'I'll help you.'

He hadn't said it right. He sounded petty, angry, resentful. And she got it. Terror turned to anger again, just like that.

'Don't you dare.'

'Dare what?'

'Dump this on me. You talked me into this. You made me come home. I'm your responsibility, Nikos. I came home because of you.'

'You came home because of the island.'

'I came home because we talked ourselves into loving this island together. If you're even thinking you need me to stay, then you need to support me every step of the way.'

'I'll support you tonight,' he said.

Beyond tonight was a place he was too fearful to think about.

CHAPTER FOUR

THE castle was a time warp.

The limousine pulled up in the castle fore-court. Athena climbed out.

Argyros, circa eighteen hundred. It was almost enough to jerk her out of the emotional mess she'd just landed herself in.

It was almost enough to make her stop thinking about Nikos.

The palace was built of the stone used throughout these islands, whitewashed once but mostly faded to its original soft grey. It was two storeys high in the centre, with long single storey wings at either end. The garden was overgrown to the point of riot. Vast wisteria vines gnarled their way over the buildings like great knots on ancient gift wrapping. There were olive trees, bougainvillea, wild daisies and clumps of blue and yellow irises—a riot of colour. The palace looked half buried by garden—a fantastic wilderness.

And behind the castle was the backdrop of the sea. As a child she'd heard the palace had the best swimming beach on the island, but who knew?

She'd never been in these grounds. The castle had been protected by vast stone walls for as long as she could remember. Guard dogs were said to roam at night.

Giorgos had hardly ever come here but he'd deemed it his. What was his he held, fiercely.

'So who does this belong to now?' she whispered to Nikos as she stood in the forecourt, feeling stunned, feeling the warmth of the Mediterranean sun on her face, hearing the wash of the sea under the cliffs.

'The Crown,' Nikos said briefly. 'That would be you. Unless you abdicate. Then it goes to Demos. He's been staying here since Giorgos died—since he phoned you and you told him he could have it. I told him you were coming back and he had to vacate.'

She gulped. 'I hadn't thought...' she whispered. 'Demos must hate me.'

'He hates me, too,' Nikos said, but he touched her arm lightly, in a gesture of reassurance which was supposed to be steadying—and strangely was. 'But we needn't feel guilty. Somehow he wheedled his way into the King's favour. Giorgos left him a personal fortune. Sadly for Demos, a fortune will never be enough.'

There was so much here to take in… She was fighting to understand it.

Meanwhile staff were waiting, lined up as if in some period play. The women were wearing uniforms that were grim-as-death black. The men wore black too, alleviated only by high starched collars in pristine white. In this Mediterranean paradise they looked…ridiculous.

'You need to meet your staff,' Nikos said, and she thought about backing into the limo and slamming the door. This was scarier than scary.

'You're kidding me, right? I can't employ these people.'

'Maybe you can't,' he said neutrally. 'Giorgos kept the castle fully staffed. Demos intended to sack them and modernise the place, but now it's your call.'

'They can't like working here.' She looked

again at the uniforms, at the stoical faces, at their ramrod straight posture. 'Looking like this…'

'Looks don't matter,' he said briefly. 'Apart from a struggling fishing industry, there's very little employment.'

Her head was starting to spin. Nikos knew this place. She didn't. It should be Nikos in charge. But he was giving her information only, and waiting for her to act as she willed.

Waiting for her to fail? Certainly he was judging her.

Anger stirred. She could do this. She would. She was *not* going to fail in front of Nikos.

The staff were in two formal lines. Not a muscle was moving. They looked almost like waxworks. 'Can I afford to pay them?' she demanded.

'The royal coffers are at your disposal,' Nikos said neutrally. 'They're overflowing.'

'How can they be overflowing? I though we were broke.'

'Giorgos taxed everything. Once a year he cleaned out the Argyros accounts and moved the money to Sappheiros. It's been nine months since they've been cleared, and Alexandros is shifting what funds he knows are ours back.

You'll need to start road repairs, harbour deepening, the infrastructure. You can provide employment and make this a better place to live in the process.'

'But I'm a fashion editor,' she said and to her horror, she heard herself beginning to wail. 'I can't do this!'

'Your staff are waiting,' Nikos said. He was holding Christa's hand. Standing apart. 'Set Oscar down—hold him by the leash,' he told Nicky. 'Your mother needs to meet the staff, and if you intend to live here then you need to meet them, too.'

'Am I going to live here?' Nicky gazed around in awe. 'Cool!'

'It is cool,' Nikos said gravely. 'I'm not sure if your mother thinks so.'

'I don't think so.' She was fighting for control. She was taking in the crumbling façade of a once magnificent palace. The derelict gardens. Twenty people lined up to see what she would do.

'Do I have a choice?' she muttered.

'No.'

'Fine, then,' she snapped. She was being thrown

in at the deep end, like it or not. She had no choice but to swim. 'I can be a princess if I need to.'

He smiled at that. 'Of course you can.'

'Okay,' she muttered.

'Well, then…'

'Well, then.' She took a deep breath. She braced her shoulders and stepped forward. She ignored the sensation of Nikos at her back, watching her. Judging her?

'Hi,' she said, in her best managing-the-staff voice. A voice she hadn't quite perfected. 'You know who I am. I probably should remember all of you but it's been almost ten years since I've been on the island so you need to forgive me. You'll also need to forgive me if I don't get things right—the things I'm supposed to do. But three things I do know, and I might as well say them now. First, not one of you will lose your job for anything except incompetence or dishonesty. Not while I'm here. Second, your salary will stay the same until I have time to review it and even then it won't drop. And finally…I hate your uniforms. Hate 'em. Who's interested in giving me suggestions for change?'

* * *

She was fabulous. She was just as he'd always imagined she'd be.

She'd been here for what—twenty minutes— and the staff were already putty in her hands. Her career had her moving with some of the world's wealthiest, most flamboyant people. She was good at her job. It showed.

He was proud of her.

How corny was that? How patronising?

He didn't have to tell her what to do, he thought. He just had to stand back and watch. And wonder.

She'd already had volunteers to redesign the uniform. She'd already said she'd like to use first names—if that was okay? The staff were already halfway to being in love with her.

Who could blame them?

'So remind me.' She was at the end of the line, looking back at him. 'The reception is at seven?'

'Yes.'

'Will my people have the details?'

My people. Just like that, she'd taken on the mantel of royalty. And once again she'd moved him to the sidelines.

'Yes,' he said shortly. 'Your staff are putting on the reception.'

'So I'll see you then?'

'Yes.'

She nodded. The eyes gazing at him were expressionless.

'We'll be happy to receive you, then,' she said.

And that was that. He'd been dismissed by royalty.

His gaze met hers and held. Then, very slowly, he nodded. And smiled.

'Until then, Your Highness,' he said softly and gave her a gentle, mocking salute. 'Off you go and introduce Oscar to his new home.'

It took all the courage in the world to watch him go—not to call him back—to stop herself whimpering in terror. But this role was hers. She'd returned to the island as Crown Princess. She had to take the responsibility.

Her dream as a kid—to take on this responsibility with Nikos—was just that—a dream. He'd married someone else. He'd moved on.

Somehow, she must too.

The housekeeper—Mrs Lavros—no first names here!—gave her a cursory tour of the palace, apologising over and over. 'There's not been money for repairs. We're so thankful you're finally here. We're so sorry we couldn't get it how we'd like it.' But neither Athena or Nicky—or Oscar either, for that matter—minded shabby.

'Ooh, it's cool,' Nicky said, and Athena gazed in awe at the vast chandelier in the bedchamber they'd just been ushered into and had to agree. This was the King's bedchamber, with a smaller bedroom leading off to the side. 'The smaller room's for the King's valet,' Mrs Lavros told her. 'It's been years since the King's been here, but we've kept it aired. There's clean linen on the beds…'

Athena was no longer listening. She was staring out of the window at the beach that had been forbidden to mere mortals since Giorgos's ancestors had plundered this place and made it theirs.

Nicky and Oscar were already out on the terrace, scrambling through the balustrades, figuring how they could clamber down to the cliff path.

She was a princess. Did princesses…clamber?

'Has Nikos seen this?' she breathed. The beach was wide and golden, curving from headland to headland. The sea was glistening diamonds—fabulous, romantic.

'I'm not sure,' the housekeeper told her. 'But if you please, ma'am, what will you wear tonight?'

Tonight. A royal reception. *How many people?* She stopped thinking about clambering.

'Something…simple?' she ventured.

The housekeeper's face fell. 'Everyone wants to meet you,' she said. 'We so want our own princess. Prince Alexandros and Princess Lily will be here from Sappheiros, of course, and they're wonderful, but they're not our ruling family. Prince Alexandros will wear his medals,' she said wistfully. 'Don't you have a formal gown?'

It was said without much hope.

And Athena looked at her two suitcases and knew her lack of hope was justified.

She'd packed for four weeks and she'd travelled light. She'd brought one formal little black dress.

Nikos should have warned her. *Nikos should have warned her about the reception*, she thought again, feeling anger build.

But…

But.

Prince Alexandros and Princess Lily would be here.

And…this was really huge…Nikos would be here as well.

Nikos, who'd fathered a child to another woman before she'd left the island. Nikos, who'd married Marika. Nikos, who she'd thought she loved with all her heart. Who'd finally, dreadfully, taught her not to trust…anyone.

He'd thrown her in the deep end here—*but she would not sink.*

He hadn't warned her. He'd expect her to be… ordinary.

She glanced at her watch. It was still only midday. She had seven hours. Could she?

Nikos would be here.

She would be a princess.

Nothing to it, she thought, mentally spitting on her hands and getting down and dusty. She wasn't fashion editor of one of the world's biggest glossies for nothing.

'Mrs Lavros, if my cellphone doesn't work here then I need a landline,' she said. 'And the Internet. I need help to become a princess and I need it fast.'

* * *

She didn't come down until seven-thirty. She almost didn't come down then.

She was listening to Nicky read. She and Nicky had changed reader/listener roles about two years back when he'd decreed her choice of stories was boring. Since then this had become her special time of day—to quieten nerves, to remind herself what was important, to focus solely on the two of them.

And this night she needed her quiet time more than she'd ever needed it in her life. This night she was terrified. For the moment she went downstairs she turned into a princess.

Nicky was reading from a manual for a Model T Ford. Gripping stuff. Much more gripping than what was happening downstairs.

But she couldn't stay up here for ever. Finally the housekeeper appeared. 'Ma'am, it's Nikos,' she said apologetically. 'He says if you're not downstairs in two minutes he'll come up and carry you down. And I think he means it.'

'You'd better go, Mama,' Nicky said. 'Nikos is really strong.' He smiled shyly at the house-keeper. 'Nikos is my Papa.'

'He's your…' The housekeeper's chin sagged. 'Well…'

'Mama just told me today,' Nicky said, proud of the effect he'd created. 'Christa is my sister.'

'Well,' the housekeeper said again. 'I can't say I didn't wonder when I saw you, but… Well.' She surveyed Athena with growing concern. 'Oh, my dear, Demos will hate it. You'll need to be so careful. But you need to get tonight over with first. You look lovely. You do us proud. But…if you don't want the father of your child to carry you forcibly down the staircase, then you'd best come now.'

Nikos was close to being out of his mind. What was Athena playing at, keeping them waiting? And she should have a gown. He hadn't thought of it until everyone had arrived, but every woman here was in an evening gown. His friend, Prince Alexandros, and his wife, Princess Lily, looked positively regal.

But it was Athena who should be a princess tonight, he thought. Dammit, he should have warned her. She'd be a real Cinderella among this splendour. And if she thought he'd orchestrated it so that she looked shabby… Anger wouldn't begin to describe it.

But there was no time left for misgivings. The housekeeper was on the stairs, looking towards him, asking a question with her gaze.

He strode through the crowd and took two steps up, so the crowd could see him. Somewhere above was Athena. He hoped like hell her dress wasn't too dowdy.

There was no time to do anything about it now. She was up on the landing, waiting for his signal to come down.

Waiting for the official introduction.

'Ladies and gentlemen,' he said in a voice that carried to every part of the vast hall. 'I give you Her Royal Highness the Princess Athena, Crown Princess Of Argyros.'

CHAPTER FIVE

THE crowd gasped as one.

Nikos stepped down and turned. And saw. And gasped himself.

She took his breath away.

She took away the breath of every man and woman in the crowded hall. Nikos had never seen her more beautiful.

He'd never seen anyone so beautiful.

She looked to be almost gliding down the stairs. One elegant hand rested on the balustrade to steady herself. Her hand was gloved, long and elegant and beautiful.

And her dress…

Her gown was shimmering silk brocade in rich, deep crimson. Its tiny capped sleeves were slipped to just off her shoulders, and the neckline dropped to show the glorious swell of her beautiful breasts. Her bodice was embroidered, red-black on the deeper crimson, and laced from breast to waist with slivers of silver thread.

From her hips the gown flared into fold on glorious fold of the same richly embroidered fabric, falling to her feet. The skirt was slashed at the front, showing a soft silk underskirt, black, shot with crimson.

Magnificent didn't begin to describe it.

She stepped slowly down the stairs, beneath the great central chandelier, as if she was aware of dramatic effect. Her gown shimmered in the light cast by a thousand crystals above her head.

There were diamonds at her throat and more at her ears. Her shoes were crimson stilettos to match her gown, studded with more diamonds still. Her beautiful black curls were caught in a simple twisting knot, tied with the same silver thread that laced her bodice.

She was an exquisite portrait. She was a royal princess.

She was the Crown Princess Athena, come home to claim her throne.

Around him there were gasps of delight, amazement, disbelief, and the gasps gave way to applause.

Nikos knew why. From the uncertainty of the past months, finally the islanders could glimpse their future. These people would be deeply appreciative of this grand gesture; deeply grateful that their princess was taking up her throne.

Thena.

No. Not Thena. This was Crown Princess Athena, a woman now so far out of his league that suddenly he felt…as if he had no place here.

'What the hell…? Where did she get that dress?' It was Demos, standing beside him, his face a picture of apoplectic fury. 'How long's she been planning this? She told me…'

'She told you she wasn't interested in ruling the island,' Nikos said, his gaze never leaving Athena. Where *had* she got the gown? It surely hadn't been in one of the small cases she'd brought here with her.

Wherever it had come from, it was perfect.

And the islanders were dumbfounded.

Athena had effectively been brought up in isolation. Families who'd shown her friendship had been harshly warned off by Giorgos. That she had turned out so full of spirit was a testament to her strength, and to her courage.

Her mother had home-schooled her, on orders from Giorgos, so Nikos hadn't met her until they'd been eight years old. He'd been bird-nesting—not stealing eggs, just observing, trying to reach the highest nests on the craggy island cliffs. She'd looked up at him from below, and he'd said, 'Dare you.' To his astonishment she'd come right on up. On the way down she'd cut her knee. Regardless of her protests, he'd taken her home so his mother could fix it.

He remembered she'd stopped outside his back door. 'I'm not allowed into people's houses.'

'Why not?' he'd demanded, astonished.

'The King says I'm not allowed.'

And he remembered his mother's reaction. She'd come out, breathing fire.

'The King doesn't command who comes into my kitchen,' she'd retorted. 'Welcome to my home, my love. Nikos, bring her in. Oh, look at your poor knee.'

Annia had defied the King to marry Nikos's father and, where Athena was concerned, she defied him again.

'You stay friends with her, Nikos. Giorgos can rant all he wants—he won't scare us.'

He looked at her now and thought Giorgos had been right to be worried. She was truly regal.

Princess Lily tucked her hand through Nikos's arm. 'Doesn't she look lovely?' she breathed.

'She does.' There was no denying such a truth.

'Why is Demos looking like thunder?'

'He thought Athena didn't want the Crown. He thought it was his for the taking.'

'He's scary,' Lily said, watching Demos shove through the crowd and leave. 'He came to see Alex a couple of days ago. I had a feeling…' She shivered. 'Sorry. I just thought…he seems ruthless.'

'There's nothing he can do.'

'Is there not? You look out for her,' Lily said urgently and Nikos frowned.

'What do you mean?'

'I know what people are capable of when there's money at stake,' she said. 'Be careful Nikos. The poor woman's terrified.'

'Are you kidding? She's every inch a princess.'

'You're only seeing the clothes,' she said and sounded disappointed in him.

What was there to see but the clothes?

A lot. He knew—a lot. But hell, it hurt to think that.

'Then there's your son,' Lily said, and he stilled.

'I beg your pardon?'

'Your son.' She was all seriousness now. 'Alex says rumours flew from the time people saw him at the ship. He says the age is right and you and Athena were lovers. No?'

'I…' What the hell…? 'Yes.'

'Then there's another reason to take care of your princess. Your son is now heir to the throne. Any threat to Athena would also be directed at him. Have you thought of that?'

No. No! The thought poleaxed him.

'Lily.' Alexandros was ushering Athena forward. 'Princess Athena, may I present my wife, Princess Lily.'

Lily smiled, then, astonishingly, dropped into a deep curtsey.

'There's no need for curtseys,' Athena said, sounding breathless, bordering on appalled.

'There certainly is,' Lily said. 'If you're about to take on the role of Crown Princess, you need every bit of respect you can get. Nikos, bow or something.'

'We're expected in the great hall,' Nikos growled. 'Princess Athena's kept the kitchen waiting. I hope dinner's not spoiled.'

Which earned him a glance of gentle reproof from Lily. 'Princess Athena's permitted to keep anything she wants waiting,' she said grandly. 'Including you, Nikos. Take the lady's hand and lead the way.'

She was seated in the centre of the head table, at a royal reception just for her. It was almost too much to take in.

To her left was Nikos, then Alexandros and then Lily. They were chatting as old friends. She'd love to be included.

But on her right was the Archbishop, talking and drinking at an alarming rate. He spoke in theological platitudes, and any attempt she made to make the conversation more general—to include Nikos, or to talk to the woman on the other side of him—saw the platitudes grow louder.

Being royal was suddenly boring.

She pecked desultorily at her dinner, not hungry, but then Nikos leaned over and murmured into her ear, ignoring the Archbishop's monotone; 'Thena, the kitchen staff have worked themselves into a lather getting this meal ready tonight. There hasn't been a royal reception on this island for twenty years. I need to tell you that they're likely to fall on their kitchen knives if you don't eat your dinner.'

She stared at him, astonished, and saw he was serious. And she had no comeback. He was already talking again with Alexandros.

Okay, she'd eat her dinner. She'd listen to the Archbishop. She'd be a good princess.

What was she letting herself in for?

She might look like a princess. She didn't feel like one.

Nikos was simply dressed in a black suit, beautifully cut, with a crisp white linen shirt. Alexandros was wearing full royal regimentals.

They looked like two princes, she thought. They *were* two princes. By right, if not by birth.

This Crown should belong to Nikos.

Finally the Archbishop paused for breath. He rose, a little unsteadily, and headed towards the bathroom.

Alexandros rose and slipped into his seat.

Once upon a time Alexandros had been her

friend as well as Nikos's friend. Once upon a time, when life had been innocent.

'I'm sorry about this,' he said softly. 'Nikos is throwing you in at the deep end.'

'This should be him—not me.'

He smiled and shook his head. 'He works behind the scenes, our Nikos. His mother's done an extraordinary amount for this island and so has Nikos. But they do it quietly and with no fuss.'

Another woman had made an almost unseemly rush to fill Alexandros's vacant chair beside Nikos. Nikos smiled a welcome at her. The woman simpered.

'Does he have a girlfriend?' Athena asked Alexandros, before she could help herself.

'Not seriously. Lots of short-term encounters but little more. I don't think he's ever got over Marika.'

'That was nine years ago.'

'How long does it take after a bad marriage to trust yourself to a good one?' Alex asked quietly. 'To learn to trust another after such betrayal…?'

They were quiet for a moment. Watching Nikos. Watching the woman inch her chair closer.

'You and he…' he said softly. 'You know, we all thought it'd work.'

'Me included,' she said before she could stop herself.

'Marika was a very attractive woman. And Nikos was very young.'

'The same age as me. Nineteen.'

'So maybe you need to forgive each other? Especially…' He hesitated and then obviously decided to be frank. 'Especially if you have a son.'

'I don't need to forgive Nikos.' She looked at Alex full-on. 'Nikos gave me my son. I regret nothing.'

'So if he forgives you…'

'He'll have it flung back in his face.'

The Archbishop was back, waiting for his chair. She turned to him and smiled sweetly.

'I'm glad you're back. Where were we?'

Nikos could do nothing but watch.

This dinner was interminable. Alexandros had abandoned him to talk to others. The woman hanging on his words was driving him crazy. He wanted out of here.

He could go. But that would mean not watching Thena, and he was mesmerised by her.

He sat and watched. He responded to the laughter and noise around him. The islanders were jubilant that they had their princess home.

He'd brought her home. He'd done his job. He should leave.

Coffee was served. An orchestra, playing gently in the background until now, raised its volume and struck up a waltz.

This had been prearranged. Alexandros was to lead Athena onto the dance floor. Alexandros, in full ceremonial uniform, was every inch a prince.

As Athena was every inch a princess.

In moments she and Alexandros were swirling round the floor with skill and grace. If Lily hadn't been sitting on the sidelines he'd have been jealous.

Jealous? He didn't want any part in this goldfish bowl of royalty. He needed to support Thena from a distance—nothing more.

The waltz ended. There was a moment's pause and he thought they were about to dance another. But Alex whispered something to Athena and strode back to Lily.

Athena stood alone for a moment, as if considering. And then she walked deliberately back to the head table, so she was standing right before him.

'Nikos, it's thanks to you that I'm here tonight,' she said steadily, clearly, so all the room could hear. 'The Prince Alexandros tells me you've taken care of this island—you've worked ceaselessly behind the scenes to protect the islanders from the worst excesses of the old monarchy. I thank you, and I ask you to do me the honour of this dance.'

She was play-acting, he thought. She'd swept down those stairs in her magnificent dress and she'd assumed the mantle of royalty.

Her words to him were those of a Crown Princess, a woman who knew her place in the world and assumed the respect of her birthright.

He'd be proud of her if he wasn't so bewildered.

If he wasn't so angry.

For there was still anger, simmering underneath. There was still Nicky's birth to sort. But now wasn't the time. Not when she was holding out her hand.

There was nothing to do but to take it.

'I'd be honoured, Your Highness,' he told her, and her control ended. It was he who led her back onto the dance floor. It was he who took her into his arms and led her into a waltz.

They could do this.

One wet winter when school was out and Athena was a constant presence, Annia had declared enough with the television and the card games.

'One day, if the gods look favourably on us, you may eventually rule this island,' she'd told Athena. 'And Nikos may well help you. So you need to learn to act as royals.'

So his mother had taught them their royal history, taught them their ancient rights, taught them protocol—and she'd also taught them to dance.

He stepped onto the dance floor, he took Athena into his arms and the years disappeared. They might as well be back in his mother's sitting room, with her complaining on the sidelines... 'Smooth, Nikos, smooth, hold her as if she's precious, not a sack of potatoes...'

Hold her as if she's precious...

How could he help but do that? She was exquisite. Her skirts were swirling around him as she melted into his arms, and he let the dance take them where they willed.

The smell of her… The feel of her…

It felt as if it was yesterday that they'd walked hand in hand over every inch of this island, swearing eternal love, swearing they could never look at another.

She was the most beautiful woman…the most beautiful princess…

The waltz ended but another began, as if the orchestra knew this was no time for interruption.

He had his Thena in his arms again. It felt as natural as life itself.

'It should be you taking the Crown,' she whispered. 'You deserve it.'

The moment—the magic—was broken. He felt it slip away with infinite regret.

'I deserve nothing, Princess.'

'Don't call me that.'

'It's what you are.'

'For four weeks.'

He almost misstepped. He'd have no excuse because dancing with Thena was like breathing.

'You can't leave,' he said. 'You know that.'

'I make up my own mind.'

'As you did last time. Walking away…'

'I believe I ran,' she said. She was smiling, a gentle smile that would have everyone thinking she was enjoying a light conversation with him.

'There was nothing to run from,' he said angrily.

'Oh, but there was,' she said, her smile not slipping. 'And I didn't know the half of it. I should have run much sooner.'

'You're not making sense.'

'Then aren't we a match?' she said.

They danced on. Other couples were joining them on the floor. He had to think of something to say. Anything.

'Where did you get your gown?' he tried.

'You like it?' She sounded strained to breaking point. 'It's worth over ten thousand dollars, which is a fraction of what these diamonds are worth.'

'What the hell…' His brow snapped down in confusion. 'You've managed to get your hands on the royal exchequer?'

Her eyes flashed fire. Somehow her feet kept moving, her smile stayed in place, but daggers could be less lethal than the look she gave him.

'I must have,' she said, and he could see that the effort it cost to keep her smile in place was almost superhuman. 'After all, I only have weeks to strip the place bare.'

'Thena…'

'Nikos,' she snapped. 'You know me better than this.'

'I don't know you.'

She didn't respond. They circled the dance floor, twice, three times more, and the music came to an end.

'Thank you,' she said stiffly and let her hands drop from his. He was aware of a sharp stab of loss. Quickly suppressed. Let's not let emotions get in the way here, he told himself.

But they already had.

'It was my pleasure,' he said, just as formally.

But she wasn't finished with him. 'I'm a fashion editor,' she said coldly, formally. 'I know the value of product placement. So I let it be known that the new Princess Athena of Argyros would be presented to the public for the first time tonight. The fashion houses' marketing teams know me. They know I can carry clothes—see, there are advantages in not eating crepés and soufflés. So they moved fast, flying clothes and jewellery from Athens this afternoon. I get to send them all back, but not before I'm photographed by the world's press—which, if you look to the balcony, also seem to be present. So I've organised my clothes, Nikos, and I've organised them myself. I'd never touch the island coffers. I never will.'

And then she added a more hesitant trailer.

'And Nikos, my feelings for you are messing with my ability to do this job. If this is to work then I need to separate them.'

'You want me to leave you alone?'

'That's it.'

'When you have my son?'

'He's not your son unless you earn the right to call him that.'

'What's that supposed to mean?'

'I don't have a clue,' she said and sighed, and then repinned her smile and turned around to a middle-aged lady who'd clearly been aching to talk to her.

Audience over.

It was so hot in here. She felt as if she was suffocating.

This dress was fabulous but it required a

serious waist. She had lacing not only on the dress but also on the less than glamorous under-garment underneath. Move over, Scarlett O'Hara, she thought grimly as the night wore on. What women put up with in the name of vanity!

But the dress, the diamonds, the effort she'd gone to, were working. There were cameras everywhere. She knew the world's press. The glossy magazines liked nothing better than royalty on their front covers. So be it. She'd done the glamorous bit as a clear signal that she was a real princess.

It was a signal to Demos to lay off. It was a signal to Nikos that she was up to the task.

She was dancing with one islander after another. They were treating her with awe. What a difference a frock makes, she thought ruefully. When she was a child these men and women had obeyed the King's ruling and had nothing to do with her.

Only Nikos and his mother had defied the King.

Nikos... He was dancing too, with one beau-tiful woman after another. Mr Popularity.

That was unfair, she conceded. She'd been here less than a day, but already she was being told how much Nikos had done for this island. He'd fought Giorgos every step of the way.

But…she was his tool, she thought bleakly, as the night wore on. She was a tool for Nikos to use in his fight to save the island. And as for the past… How much of that had been real and how much had it been Nikos's desire to rule this island as he wanted it to be ruled?

The dancing ended. She needed air. She left the ballroom and the crowd parted before her as if she was…royalty.

Could she ever get used to this?

The room next to the ballroom was the great hall where dinner had been served. It was deserted now, cleared and empty. But its vast windows looked onto a balcony, and the balcony looked over the sea.

She walked out and stood at the parapet, gazing out over the ocean. Breathing the night air. Breathe in, breathe out. Try to relax.

She smelled the salt breeze from the sea. There was the scent of flowers she hadn't seen or smelled for ten years.

She loved this island. Loved it.

'What the hell do you think you're playing at?'

She whirled and it was Demos, portly and flaccid and simmering with obvious rage. He walked out and slammed the door behind him. 'Do you seriously think you can get away with this?'

'With what?'

'It's mine,' he said fiercely, stepping towards her with an intent that frightened her. 'Giorgos always meant it to go to me.'

'Giorgos no longer has a say in how this island will be ruled. It's in the hands of the…'

'The gods? Don't give me that. You're not wanted here. You promised me…'

'I meant the people. And I didn't promise you anything.'

'Liar.'

'You lied to me,' she said evenly. 'You said you cared for this island. Now I find it was just greed.'

He was so close to her she could feel his breath. He was pushing his body into her space, so her back was hard against the parapet. 'You left this island to have a kid. Nikos's kid. They're all saying it. You think we want a woman like you to run the island?'

'I care for the island more than you do.'

'You don't know what care is.' He closed his eyes. Regrouped. 'Okay. Here's another solution. You know how much these diamond mines are worth? We can split it. You don't want to live here. Neither do I—it's the pits—but someone has to. You go back to your life in New York and I'll take over. I'll do what has to be done and we'll cut the profits. Fifty-fifty. You can't say fairer than that.'

'Demos,' she said, trying desperately to keep her voice steady, 'I'm not opening the mines.'

'You might have to.'

'I don't know what you mean.'

'There are ways,' he said viciously. 'You care about your kid, don't you. It'd be a shame if anything happened to him. You can't watch him all the time. You go back to Manhattan and he'll be safe again.'

She felt cold and she felt sick.

'You can't hurt us,' she managed.

And he simply smiled. And he raised a hand to hit her.

Only…he didn't. She was backed as far as she could, putting her hands up in a futile attempt to prevent a blow, but the sweeping hand didn't reach her.

A dark shape had sprung from the shadows as if it had always been there. Demos's hand was held before it had a chance to find its mark.

Demos twisted, lashing out with his boots, moving so the shadow was now in the light.

Nikos.

'How dare you touch her?' He let Demos's hand drop as if it was slime. Demos struck out again, but Nikos was before him. He punched, so hard that Demos sprawled backward, crashing over an ornate chair, falling, hitting the ground with a sickening thud. Lying there for one long moment while Thena thought, dear God, he's killed him.

Nikos didn't say a word. His hand came out and took Thena's, holding hard.

An oath came from the tiled floor. Not dead, then.

Nikos tugged her hard against him, putting her slightly behind him, his body between her and her cousin. He watched in grim silence as Demos struggled to his feet.

Demos straightened, swore again and looked at Nikos with murder in his eyes. If he'd had a gun, Athena thought with a shiver of pure dread, then Nikos would be dead. Or if he'd been wearing Alexandros's ceremonial sword…

'What is she to you?' he snarled to Nikos. 'This has nothing to do with you.'

'Princess Athena is the mother of my son,' Nikos said and his voice made Athena shudder. It was as cold as ice, rigid, formal and grim. 'You just threatened my son. And…' he tugged Athena closer '…you were about to strike my woman. I'll defend what's mine, and this woman and her son are mine. Hear me well, Demos, for I mean every word. Get yourself out of this palace and off the royal grounds. If you're seen within sight of Princess Athena or her son again you'll be thrown off the island, never to return.'

Then he turned his back on Demos as if he had no interest in him at all—and he took Athena into his arms.

CHAPTER SIX

ATHENA stayed right where she was, held tight against Nikos.

She was shuddering so hard she couldn't stop, and it was easier to stay than to pull away. For who wanted to pull away?

She no longer knew what Demos was doing. She couldn't see—Nikos didn't let her see. She was aware of heavy breathing, of his sinister presence. Nikos must be watching him, but her face was buried against his chest.

'Leave,' Nikos said again, quietly. There was a loaded silence, then a muttered oath of such invective it took her breath away—and Demos was gone.

'He hates me,' she whispered, feeling ill.

'He doesn't love and he doesn't hate,' Nikos said. 'He wants. He wants wealth and more wealth. Thena…' He put her away from him, holding her at arm's length.

'Thena, you're standing between Demos and a fortune.'

'I don't want it.'

'That's why I brought you home,' he said softly. 'Because you'd never want it. I knew that about you when you were eight years old, and people can't change so much. Demos was greedy from the start. He'll destroy these islands. You can face up to him but…'

'But I don't want to.'

'No. And you also say you're going back to New York. I understand your career is important to you. You put it before the island once before—and I understand you'll do it again. But these people want a figurehead, Thena.'

'I'm not a figurehead. I'm just me.'

He shook his head at that one. 'Look at you,' he said, smiling wryly, and once more he had her at arm's length. 'You're stunning. You're every inch a princess. You're who the people want.'

'I don't want to be royal.'

'Sometimes what we want and don't want

doesn't come into it,' he said softly. 'Demos isn't alone, you know. There are heavies behind him.'

'Heavies?'

'Yes.'

'Like…armed thugs. People who could hurt my Nicky?' She whirled away from him and headed for the door but his hand came out and caught her. 'Let me go.' She wrenched back but he didn't release her. He tugged her closer so her breasts were against his chest. He had her by one arm, holding it about her, tugging her in so she was pulled tight against him.

'Where are you going?'

'I'm going to Nicky.' But he was letting her go nowhere.

'He's safe. I've had security guards watch you both from the moment you set foot on the island.' He smiled, apologetic. 'Longer, in fact. Even in Manhattan. You lessened the risk by telling Demos he could have the throne but even then we didn't trust him.'

'We?'

'There are many islanders whose livelihoods hang on you inheriting,' he said. 'Demos's heavies don't have it all their own way. For if Demos succeeds…'

'You really think he'd hurt Nicky?'

'Yes.' It was a flat statement with no equivocation.

'Then I'm leaving. He can have it. I don't want it. Not if it puts Nicky in the slightest danger. Let me go!'

'Thena, do you really want Demos to destroy these islands?'

His voice was grave, low and urgent, and something about his tone stopped the rising hysteria, the rising panic.

This was the real Nikos. The Nikos she'd spent her teenage years with. The Nikos who cared about this place so passionately that he'd taught her to care as well.

Until she'd met Nikos she'd been taught to feel as trapped as her mother was trapped. 'We'd leave if we could afford it,' her mother had told her. 'I'm so sorry you have to stay here. I'm so sorry the royals are destroying your life as well as mine.'

That was how she'd been raised, but then along came Nikos, with his passion, his fire, his certainty that they could make things right.

She'd fallen in love with his fire.

And she heard that fire now, the sheer single-minded determination to create justice for this island, to do whatever needed to be done to achieve that end.

'I can't care,' she whispered. 'Not if Nicky's in danger. You'd feel the same if it was Christa.'

'I feel the same that it's Nicky,' he said. 'He's my son, too.'

Once again he'd taken her breath away. He was still holding her, hand to hand, his hold imparting warmth, strength and urgency.

'He's not… I mean, how can you care?'

'I would have cared for ten years if you'd let me.'

And the old anger stirred. For ten long years… 'Not one call, Nikos.'

'Not one letter, Thena.'

'Dammit, this is past history.'

'It's not. It's here and now. It's two kids we care deeply about, an island we care deeply about, and our future.'

'My future's in Manhattan.'

'You won't be safe in Manhattan. I can't protect you there. Thena, there are six diamond mines at stake. We're talking billions. That money has to be held in trust for the island for ever. It can't stay in royal hands. We need to get the royal thing sorted, the government sorted, so we can finally transfer the mines to the community. So these mines are no longer owned by one man—or one woman—but the island as a whole so they can be worked sensitively as the community needs them. You need to stay for three reasons. One, so I can protect you. Two, so we can keep the mines safe. And three…' He hesitated. 'Three, because Nikos is my son. I've missed ten years of his life, and I believe I have the right to know him now.'

This was doing her head in. The impersonal and the personal were mixing in a combination that was threatening to overwhelm her.

Nikos had been her first love. For the last ten years she'd tried to forget him, but she never could. Every man she'd dated she'd compared with Nikos and they'd fallen short.

She'd finally decided Nikos was a figment of a young girl's romantic longings. Impossible to be true, but also impossible to leave behind.

But here was the dream, come spectacularly to life. Nikos, with a body to die for, a smile to die for… And words so blunt and decisive that she believed him.

There was no reason to believe him, she told herself desperately. Christa. Remember Christa.

'Why can't I sign the diamond mines over now?' she demanded. 'Put them in a community fund or something?'

'There's no community fund. Everything's owned by the Crown.'

'Then set one up.'

'I can't set one up, Princess. Only you can do that.'

'Then I'll do it,' she said wildly. 'Tomorrow. And don't call me Princess.'

'It can't be done tomorrow. You think you can just hand that amount of wealth to the town council and walk away? I need to tell you now that it would be a catastrophe. It'll take years to get this right. So how about it, Thene? Say you'll stay and let me protect you. I've told Demos I'll protect what's mine and I mean just that.'

And amazingly, infuriatingly, he was smiling. That smile was so…so… Seductive. He was seducing her with his voice and with his smile, she thought wildly.

'I'm not yours,' she managed.

'You're the mother of my son.'

Oh, great. What sort of answer was that? One that joined them at the hip for ever?

'You saw the press here tonight,' he said. 'The world has another princess. Do you think you can escape that? The press will follow you all the way to Manhattan. And so will Demos.'

'You're scaring me.'

'You need to be scared.' His smile faded. 'I'm sorry, Thena, but you need to face facts.'

'You didn't tell me these facts when you conned me into coming here,' she snapped. 'That there'd be threats to Nicky…'

'You wouldn't have come.'

'Exactly.'

'You had to come. And I will protect both you and Nicky.'

'You're still angry I didn't tell you about Nicky.'

'How can I not be?'

She wrenched her hands back so strongly that this time he did let her go. 'Well how do you think I feel? You betrayed me in the worst possible way. I thought you were my best friend as well as my lover—and nothing. Nothing!'

'It was your decision to walk away.'

'It wasn't.'

He stilled. 'What do you mean?'

But she wasn't going there. Some things were best left unsaid.

'I need to go to bed, Nikos,' she said wearily, knowing it was true. 'I'm exhausted. It's been some day.'

'You will think about what I've said?'

'I will think about it,' she said. 'Of course I'll think about it. You've scared me. You seriously think Demos could harm me? Yes, he's greedy and shallow, but he's my cousin. I don't know what you stand to gain by my staying…'

'I told you. Nicky.'

'You think I trust you enough to think that's the only reason?'

'You can trust me, Thene.'

'This is nonsense, Nikos,' she said wearily. 'Once upon a time we trusted each other, but that was a long time ago. I'm so confused I can't think straight. So let me be. Tomorrow I'll think about arrangements for when I return to Manhattan. I'll do my best to protect the island from Demos. I'll talk to lawyers—I'll do what I have to do. But trust you? How can I ever do that?'

And she turned and walked back into the ballroom, her gown swishing around her.

Leaving Nikos in the shadows, watching with troubled hooded eyes.

Knowing she was walking further into danger. Knowing there was only one real way he could protect her but to do that…to trust her that far…

Once upon a time we trusted each other…

It cut both ways.

Finally, thankfully, the interminable evening was at an end. She listened while the Archbishop made his ponderous farewells, she said a formal goodnight to those she must, and then she practically ran upstairs.

Nicky was safe. She opened the adjoining door and saw a mound in the bed by the window, draped by another mound. Nicky with Oscar on top.

He wasn't supposed to let Oscar onto the bed, but who was complaining tonight? Now, all she felt was comfort from the big dog's presence.

A shape rose from a chair beside the door and she practically yelped.

'Ma'am, it's only me.'

Mrs Lavros. Her heart thudded back into place. 'Wh…why are you here?' she stammered.

'Mr Nikos asked me to stay here,' she said. 'His instructions are that we're not to leave the little one alone.'

'What…what right does he have…?'

'No right, more's the pity. But he cares about this island so much.'

'You think…' It was hard to stop her voice from squeaking. On the second try she managed it. 'You think he should be Crown Prince?'

'Everyone knows and trusts him,' the housekeeper said solidly. 'You've been away so long… But Nikos has been here. He's always been the one we've turned to in times of trouble. He's always been ready to stand up to Giorgos. In the last few years we've been left more or less alone, thanks to Nikos. But now…you're here…and Nikos says you'll make a fine Crown Princess and I'm sure you will too, ma'am. It's Demos and his friends who Nikos worries about. He's fearful for you.'

'He shouldn't worry. I'll be fine.'

'I know you'll be fine,' the housekeeper told her. 'For Nikos is keeping you that way. He has guards in place in the corridor and out in the grounds. You're safe.'

She stared, bewildered. 'Are you kidding? He's scaring me witless.'

The housekeeper nodded. 'He said that. He said he couldn't protect you without scaring you a little. But I wouldn't be fearful. He's a good man.'

'He's been talking crazy talk tonight,' she said.

Mrs Lavros raised her brows in polite disbelief. 'Has he now? It's not something I'd credit. All I know is that whatever Nikos does there's reason for. Goodnight, ma'am. Sleep well and safely, for he'll be watching over all of us.'

She sat for a while and watched Nicky and Oscar sleep. She tried to sort the events of the day into some sort of order.

She failed. It was a weird kaleidoscope of emotions, with Nikos front and centre.

Finally, so tired she could scarcely stand, she walked into her bedroom—the King's bedchamber—and started to undress.

Uh-oh.

One of the maids had helped her dress. The gown had something akin to a corset underneath, designed to make her figure a lot more hourglass than it naturally was. There were fine bands of what was surely whalebone inserted inside.

It was laced down the back.

This gown was designed to have people help the wearer in and help the wearer out.

Here there was only her.

She struggled. She struggled some more. She was almost turning herself inside out.

It wouldn't even rip. And where were a pair of scissors when she needed them? She was in a royal palace—where did she go in a royal palace to find scissors?

There was a bell pull by the mantel. She could pull it—but how loud would it be? She might wake the whole palace.

She struggled and swore some more. She was practically breaking her neck trying to see where the lacing was. Even if she could see how it was laced, she couldn't reach.

She could wake Nicky, she thought desperately.

Right, that'd be a help. Once he went to sleep Nicky slept like the dead. She'd wake him and it'd take a cold shower to get him alert enough to unlace her.

Dammit, she could do it. If she could just reach an inch further…

There was a knock on the door.

She froze. It was two in the morning. What the…?

'Who is it?'

'Nikos.' There was no mistaking the voice. Brusque. Urgent.

Nikos. She didn't know whether to be relieved or not.

'Are you okay?' he demanded.

'Of course I'm okay,' she managed. 'Why wouldn't I be okay?'

'The security guards in the garden contacted me. They said you appeared to be in trouble.'

'I'm not.'

'They said you were struggling—that you appeared distressed.'

What the…?

She stared at the window.

And winced.

The great bay windows of her bedroom were hung with fine silken netting. That formed the first layer of curtaining. But there was a second layer. Swathes of crimson velvet were pulled back, fastened to the sides with huge golden tassels.

Oh, no.

She glanced through into Nicky's room, checking his windows.

The velvet curtains had been pulled closed.

Until now she hadn't even noticed that there were heavier curtains over the fine ones. But now… She'd been standing before the dresser, trying to see the back of her dress in the mirror.

There was a chandelier in the centre of the room, blazing with light. So she'd been standing in a netted bay window, struggling with her dress, while the chandelier shone its light behind her.

They would have been able to see…

She blushed and blushed, then blushed some more. And ached for her nice anonymous Manhattan apartment.

'I'm fine,' she managed.

'Thena, what's wrong? Is someone in there with you?'

'I'm stuck,' she said, and listened to the silence on the other side of the door.

'Stuck?' he said at last, cautiously.

'Yes, stuck. This damned dress…'

'You're stuck in your dress?'

'In my underskirt. Oh, for heaven's sake, I'll let you in, but if you dare laugh…'

'I won't…laugh,' he said, but laughter was already in his voice. Of course he'd laugh. She knew this man too well.

'Pull the curtains first,' he said, and she could still hear the laughter. 'I need to radio the men to say there's no drama, but if I enter… They can see…'

'I know what they can see.' She hauled the curtains closed with a viciousness she was feeling towards the underskirt—and towards the man in the corridor—and hauled the door open.

Nikos was no longer in his formal black suit. He was in a pair of jeans and a loose battered jacket. His hair was tousled and unkempt.

And she knew…

'They woke you up,' she said, stunned.

'They were worried.'

'I couldn't get my dress off and they contacted you?'

'It looked like…'

'I don't even want to think what it looked like,' she managed. 'Don't you dare grin.'

'I wouldn't dare.' But he was grinning.

'Are you sleeping in the palace?'

'For the time being.'

'Where's Christa?'

'With my mother.'

She stared at him blankly. He gazed back, his laughter fading.

'You really are worried about me,' she whispered.

'We really are, Princess.'

'Don't call me that.' She was close to hysterics, she thought. She was close to…

'Hey, it's not all bad.'

'Isn't it?'

'It's not.' His hands caught her shoulders and held. He was looking down at her, his dark eyes fathomless. 'Thena…'

'Don't.'

'Don't what?'

'I don't know,' she muttered, totally bewildered, backing away from his hold. 'Just unfasten this slip, will you? I'm ready to rip it but the fashion house that lent it to me would have forty fits. Besides,' she added honestly, 'I tried and it wouldn't. Why aren't you wearing a sword?'

'A sword?'

'To slice the thing open.'

'You want me to slice your underclothes off with a sword?' he said cautiously. 'I don't know. It sounds a bit…cavalier…'

'You're laughing.'

'I'm not laughing.'

'Just get it off,' she said, and then looked at his face and thought uh-oh. The royal command wouldn't work here. This was Nikos and he always had been one for trouble.

'Please,' she said before he could make another wisecrack. 'Can you unfasten it?'

'A sword would be more fun. Will you wait until I find one?'

'No! Just unlace me.'

'Okay, Princess,' he said and smiled again. 'I could never resist a damsel in distress. Even without my sword I'll rescue you. Come here.'

'N… No.'

'Sorry?'

But other sensations were surfacing here. Something about the night, the lateness. Something about how damned sexy he looked— laconic, strong and sure, dressed how she'd always known him, battered clothes, a bit unkempt. Gorgeous.

'I…I think I've changed my mind,' she stammered. 'Can you call the housekeeper?'

'You don't think I can unlace you?'

'I don't know if I trust you.'

'That's a harsh thing to say.'

She bit her lip. But she was right. She'd thought she'd known this man as well as she'd known herself. One nine-year-old daughter had put paid to that trust.

But still. This was only lacing. She trusted him enough for lacing, she conceded.

'Okay,' she said begrudgingly and his smile broadened. It was a killer smile. It was a smile to melt a woman's heart.

'Good. But if we're talking undressing here… Let's make doubly sure we lose our audience.'

He flicked the light switch. The chandelier disappeared into darkness. The only light remaining was the fire's soft glow in the grate. It hadn't been tended for hours so it was now a bed of soft-glowing coals.

It was hard to see anything by. It was hard to see Nikos by.

But she knew what he looked like. He'd been her friend for ever. He'd been her lover as well, for just a short, sweet time, but that loving had been a natural and wonderful extension of their friendship.

She hadn't forgotten any of it.

So here he was, her Nikos, in her darkened bedroom. Moving towards her with intent.

She should order him out. But it was as if this was meant, a part of who she was.

She looked up at him in the dim light, not backing away, knowing what was intended, knowing also that his intent matched hers. Knowing he knew it.

She stood, simply waiting. Simply wanting.

He took her in his arms—and he kissed her.

She froze, for a whole three seconds, while her mouth registered his touch, while her body registered his feel, while she realised what was happening and that she wanted it as much as he did.

She should push him away. If she was sensible…

But the sensible part of her was no longer connected to who she was.

For she was suddenly the Athena of ten years ago. Athena in Nikos's arms. Half of the Thena and Nikos partnership, forged when they'd been eight years old, broken but now magically come back together.

It was as if two parts of a whole had finally rejoined, fusing, so the white noise disappeared, the voices muted that said this was crazy, dangerous, stupid…

This wasn't *stupid*. This was Nikos. This was his body against hers, his mouth on hers, his hands holding her tight, tighter… Nikos, making the night disappear.

He was pulling her so close she felt she was sinking into him. Maybe part of her was, and it was sinking back where it belonged.

Crazy, crazy, crazy.

She didn't care.

Her breasts were on fire where they were touching his body, and the fire was spreading. Heat was building, starting low, moving upward, flooding her body with fierce, hot want.

Nikos.

His tongue was in her mouth, exploring, searching and she felt herself stagger. It didn't matter, for his big hands were holding her, cradling her against him, allowing no chance of her falling away from him.

She was his woman. His mouth said it. His hands said it.

Nikos, Nikos, Nikos.

She was surrendering to him. She wanted him so much. Nikos…

But then, cruelly, outside intruded. The radio at his belt crackled into life. 'You okay, boss?' It was a gruff request, full of concern.

He had to respond. She knew he did.

He pulled away with a muttered oath. 'Dammit, I should have… You're distracting me, woman.'

'Is that my fault?' she demanded, even managing to sound indignant, and he grinned. There were electric charges going off everywhere here, zinging around in the darkness like fireflies. She felt light and hot and wonderful.

She hated the voice on the radio.

'It's okay, Zak, just a wardrobe malfunction,' he said into the radio and there was a moment's static-filled silence.

Then… 'You want some help fixing it, boss?'

'I believe we have the situation…in hand,' Nikos said, and the look he gave her was pure need. The zinging started all over again, filling the room with wonder.

He replaced the radio on his belt and took her hands in his. 'Like that's done my reputation some good,' she managed.

He grinned. 'You want a reputation, you just got one.'

But the break had changed things. Just a little, but enough. The first desperate tug of attraction had pulled them together. Now common sense was returning. Just.

'You want that I should unlace this slip?' he asked.

'Yes,' she whispered. 'Then…I think you ought to leave.'

'You want me to leave?'

'Nikos…'

'Okay.' His tone was suddenly flat. 'Yeah, okay. We need to keep some sanity here.'

'I am…I *am* going back to Manhattan.'

'You can't,' he said flatly.

Here it was again, this crazy proposition. But she was too tired. It was doing her head in.

She said nothing. He looked at her for a long considering minute and finally he nodded. 'Okay, Princess. You've had enough for one day. But you do need to see sense. Meanwhile…maybe we should stay away from each other's bodies. It's making me crazy. So let's sleep on what's the sensible course of action for all of us. Your career destroyed what was between us personally. I can't believe you'll let it destroy the island as well.'

'It didn't…'

'Goodnight, Princess,' he said softly, not letting her finish, and it was as if he was closing a door on what had just passed. Locking a door and throwing away the key. 'Think about everything… Please.'

CHAPTER SEVEN

ATHENA woke as two bodies landed on her bed. Nicky and Oscar, zooming in from the other room, launching themselves on top of her, Oscar barking and Nicky whooping.

'Breakfast,' Nicky said. 'Breakfast in bed, Mama. Pancakes.'

There was a soft tap on the door.

'She's awake,' Nicky yelled and a maid appeared, holding a tray.

The maid was dressed in a lovely sapphire-coloured frock, a shirt-waister, buttoned through from throat to waist, the skirt flaring out a little but not too much, tied at the waist.

The difference from the grimly clothed servants she'd seen yesterday was astonishing.

The girl was smiling. 'Please, ma'am, I'm sorry but Nikos said we were to wake you with breakfast at ten.'

'Nikos said...' Her bemusement deepened. There were so many questions she needed answering. 'Nikos gives orders to the palace staff?'

'Yes, ma'am,' the girl said as if her question was a bit foolish. 'For the most part there was no one else to do it.'

'Nikos is a fisherman,' she said cautiously. She had her arms full of dog. Oscar had obviously missed her deeply all night—and was making up for lost time.

'Nikos has six fishing boats and employs many,' the girl said simply. 'When the King started taxing the fishermen so heavily they could no longer operate, Nikos started taking fish to the mainland. He organised funds there that Giorgos couldn't touch. In the end the only way the King could stop him was by arresting him and confiscating his boats, but somehow he found the courage to face his uncle.' She smiled wistfully. 'The islanders love him,' she said simply. 'He would make a wonderful Crown Prince.'

And then...she realised what she'd said and her eyes widened in horror. 'I didn't mean, ma'am... I mean...we believe you'll make a wonderful Crown Princess. It's just that we all know Nikos and trust him.'

Despite the apology, there was still regret in her words. Athena heard it—and she even agreed.

Nikos should be Crown Prince.

He would have been, she thought. If they'd married as they'd once planned.

Marriage to the ruler meant automatic and equal status for the spouse.

So… The thought was suddenly there. What if…?

No. There wasn't enough trust in the world to take her down that path.

Was there?

Marriage… It was such a huge concept that to take it any further seemed terrifying.

Concentrate on now, she told herself, feeling suddenly dizzy. Concentrate on what came next right now. Any more and her head might explode.

Her bed was big enough to hold a small army. Someone must have crept in earlier and rebuilt the fire. It was crackling cheerfully in the grate. The maid was pulling back the curtains. Nicky was already tucking into pancakes—made by the palace staff and brought to her in bed. The morning sun was glimmering across the terrace, and beyond the terrace was the sea.

It made her feel rich. It made her feel ostentatious. It made her feel that she had no right to be here.

'I love your uniform,' she managed, hauling herself back to reality. 'Do you like it?'

The girl smoothed her skirt with pleasure. 'Maria sewed all night. This is the first. She says if you like it she'll make more.'

'I love it,' she said with enthusiasm.

Good. Think of anything but Nikos, she told herself. Anything but Nikos.

Uniforms.

'You know, sapphire looks great on you, but some of the staff might like different colours. How about we leave the choice of colour to each person?'

'Oh,' the girl said, and flushed with pleasure. 'We'd look like a rainbow.'

'It seems there haven't been rainbows round here for a long time. It's a wonder Nikos hasn't suggested change already.'

'Oh, he has no authority to change the King's orders,' the girl said blithely. 'Or yours either, ma'am. And he never would. He knows his place.'

How had they got back to Nikos again? It seemed as if her mind was a whirlpool and, in the centre…Nikos.

Give in, she thought. Just let it come.

'And…and his place is with his fishing fleet?'

'I…yes, ma'am.' The girl didn't understand what she was asking—and who could blame her? 'He has six boats, but the one he uses is the one he built himself when he was a young man. The *Athena*.'

'He has a fishing boat called the *Athena*?' she said, stunned.

'Yes, ma'am,' the girl said and smiled. 'It's nice that he called his boat after his Princess.'

'Yes, Athena said cautiously. 'Um… Is he on his boat now?'

'I believe he left the palace before dawn.'

So…Nikos was fishing.

While she played princess.

What did princesses do all day?

She wouldn't mind going fishing. She wasn't bad at hauling up craypots herself.

'I should talk to my cousin Demos,' she said doubtfully.

'I believe Prince Demos left on the morning ferry for Athens,' the girl said and blushed. 'I…I overheard one of the security guards.'

The day spread before her. No Demos.

No Nikos.

There were probably papers she should be reading, she thought.

She glanced out of the window. The beach looked…fantastic.

'Feel like a swim, Nicky?'

Nicky had been sharing a pancake with Oscar. He paused. She'd said the magic word.

'Swim,' Nicky said cautiously. 'In the sea?'

'That's the one.'

'Yay,' he yelled, and Athena found herself smiling. Life couldn't be all bad.

Threats were a nightmare; something for the dark recesses of the night. Not for now.

Nikos had gone fishing. Long may he stay there. Just as long as he stayed out of her head.

Was he nuts to go fishing? He had a team of fishermen working for him now, and a solid fleet of boats. He hardly needed to fish himself.

But he hadn't slept. If he couldn't sleep he might as well work.

At least Demos had left the island. It seemed he was on his way to Athens, maybe to confer with lawyers to try to figure a way around Thena's right to rule.

He wouldn't get answers he'd like. Athena's right to the throne was inviolate.

As long as she stayed safe.

But if she left as she said she would… Anything could happen to her back in Manhattan. He couldn't watch over her.

And Nicky… How could he get to know his son if he left? And Demos would still be a threat to him as well.

What the hell to do…

He knew what he wanted to do. He wanted to lift them up, sweep them under his own protection, place them in his house and leave them there.

But he had to concede it wasn't just common sense that was telling him to do that. It was sheer unequivocal lust.

He wanted Thena. He'd wanted her ten years ago and, astonishing or not, his desire was greater than ever. But she'd walked away once because of her career and now she was threatening to walk away again.

Was one career so important? He loved fishing, but would he put it aside if the island's livelihood was in doubt?

Of course he would.

But Thena wasn't him. Once he'd thought he'd known her, but her leaving had shocked his foundations to the core. Not telling him about Nicky had shaken him even further.

He no longer trusted her. And she didn't trust him. He knew why.

But, regardless, it had been Thena's decision to walk away. She hadn't known about Christa or Marika then. So the choice had been hers. One phone call from her and his life would have followed a completely different course.

But it hadn't. And now he had Christa. His little daughter who he'd decided years ago would be protected against everything. *Everything.*

Lay craypots, he told himself sharply. Work with your hands and not with your head.

So he laid craypots. But he just so happened to have taken his trawler around the headland, into the cove below the palace. He could watch the palace from here. He could see the beach.

So he was still laying craypots when they

came down for a swim. Athena and Nicky, followed by Oscar.

Unashamedly he found his field glasses and watched. They were skipping down the path leading from the palace. Laughing at their dumb dog. Wearing swimsuits and carrying towels.

Where were his men?

He scoured the cliffs and found two, watching from above. Another was melting into the shadows in the cliff below.

He relaxed. She was safe. She wouldn't be aware of the security men. She could enjoy her swim.

They'd reached the beach. She'd thrown off her towel and was chasing Nicky into the surf.

She was wearing a bikini. Red. He could see every curve of her delectable body.

He wanted her so much… How the hell was he going to control this?

They were swimming now. Nicky was almost as strong a swimmer as his mother. They were stroking out from the shallows, while Oscar barked objections from the shore.

His heart was doing weird things in his chest. He shouldn't be watching.

His son.

His woman?

For the first time since Nikos had found her in Manhattan, she felt at peace.

She'd swum in these waters—not in this cove, but in one like it—as a child. She loved it. In Manhattan, ocean swimming was out of the question, but she used public pools and she'd taught Nicky to swim almost before he could walk. Any time she could she'd take him swimming, and now her salary was good there'd been a couple of magic holidays where she'd been able to introduce him to waves.

He swam as well as she did.

And he loved this. She watched his face as he hit the water—watched his incredulous delight.

She knew he'd been torn since they'd arrived. Telling him Nikos was his papa had pleased him on one level, but he was also confused. He'd responded well initially, but she needed to follow up.

Or…Nikos needed to follow up, she acknowledged, and that scared her. Nikos getting to know her son.

Nikos getting to know *his* son.

They both needed distraction. 'I'll race you to the headland,' she called, and he grinned and put his head down and swam. She could still beat him, she thought, but not for long.

He had Nikos's long, lean body. He had a start on her now—and she'd have a struggle to catch him.

But then… The sound of an incoming boat reverberated through the water. She felt it rather than heard it.

She lifted her head to see…

Nikos was about to bait a craypot when he heard it. He paused, shielding his eyes from the sun. What the…?

A speedboat was coming in from the north. Fast. This type of boat was almost unknown on Argyros. No islander had money for a boat that didn't pay its keep, and this one looked like a toy of the wealthy. It was built for speed, and right now the thing was almost airborne.

As it grew nearer the noise was almost deafening. It was heading across the entrance to the cove, as if its skipper was intent on circumnavigating the island as some dumb speed challenge.

He didn't like it.

He didn't like it one bit.

Instinctively he reached for the throttle. He was hauling on the rudder. And suddenly he was yelling.

For he knew. Suddenly, sickeningly, he knew.

'Thena,' he yelled. He was hauling his boat around with all the power at his disposal, yelling into the radio. 'Get them out of the water. Get them out…'

Maybe he was mistaken. Maybe they'd pass.

But he was right. At the last minute the boat swerved in towards the beach, its engine still screaming. There were two men crouched low. Dressed in black. Hooded.

There wasn't an identifying mark on the vessel.

All this he saw in the split second before the boat had passed. Heading straight past him, into the cove.

With one aim.

'Thena,' he yelled again, but his boat wouldn't pull round fast enough. The fishing trawler was too big, she wasn't powerful enough, he couldn't get to the woman he loved in time to save her…

* * *

She'd just reached Nicky. She caught his foot and tugged.

He spluttered and came up laughing. 'You little fish,' she said and hugged him—and then glanced sideways at the source of the noise.

And grabbed Nicky, hauling him against her. They hung together in the water, watching. They were close to a beach. They were hardly out of the shallows.

The boat would veer away.

It wouldn't. Instead it turned slightly…

'Dive,' she screamed to her son. 'Dive deep, Nicky, now!'

Nikos was gunning the trawler towards the shore with a speed he'd never pushed it to before. He was yelling uselessly into the radio.

His men were out from their cover, yelling towards the speedboat.

Running down the cliff face, along the beach. Too late. Too late.

And then the boat was spinning, making a one hundred and eighty degree turn almost on its own axis, and where there'd been woman and child there was nothing.

He was so close… So close…

The wash of the speedboat as it turned had churned the waves, making it impossible to see. It must have hit them square on. There was no sign of them, nothing…

The boat was screaming back past him. One of the hooded figures in the boat had a gun. Nikos saw it, he jerked sideways and felt the zing of a bullet, just touching his cheek.

The other figure grabbed his companion, gesticulating back at the water where they'd come from. Deciding whether to sweep in again.

There was still no sign of them… Dear God, there was no sign.

Nikos was where he'd last seen them now, searching the water. Men were still yelling from the beach. Yelling at him. Yelling at the speedboat. He glanced aside, half expecting it to scream in once more.

Men were wading into the shallows. His men were armed. He saw Zeb raise his rifle and fire.

It was enough. The speedboat's motor screamed to full throttle and it blasted its way out of the cove and around the headland and away.

He didn't see it go. He wasn't looking for the boat.

He was looking for his Thena and he was looking for his son.

Nicky was better than she was at this game. They'd played it over and over—who could go furthest underwater. For the last six months he'd been able to go almost a quarter length of the pool further than she could.

He was one bright kid and he'd caught the urgency. He was pushing himself through the water beside her, at right angles to the boat, towards the rocks.

She'd go as far as he would. She'd go…

Not as far.

She shoved him away from her, gesticulated for him to keep going, and she burst upward.

Into sunlight.

Into air.

The noise of the boat was receding. Instead she heard the heavy thrum of a bigger engine.

She wouldn't go down again. Nicky would surface in seconds—dear God, please let him get far enough away so she could distract whoever it was…the maniac…

A boat was coming nearer. Not a speedboat. Something much bigger. Much more solid.

A fishing boat.

Nikos.

She was there. He saw her surface, glance at his trawler, look frantically around, searching for the threat, searching for her son.

Hell, where was Nicky? The propeller… He cut the motor to silence.

The men on the beach were still shouting.

'Thena,' he called, and she swung round to face him.

'Nicky,' she screamed, and her voice was filled with terror.

But thirty yards away the surface of the water broke. A child's face popped up.

'Miles further,' he yelled to his mother.

And then he burst into tears.

It took him seconds to haul them up, Nicky first, hugging him hard and fast, and Thena after. He hauled her on board, she slithered out of his arms and grabbed Nicky and she held him as if she'd never let go. He looked at them both—Thena and his son—and his world changed.

His trawler was wallowing in the swell close to shore. It'd be grounded if he let it drift any further. It didn't matter—who cared about a boat? He crouched on the deck with them. He put his arms around them and held.

And he knew…

Whatever else happened, whatever Thena decided, whatever course things took from this day, this was his family.

A month ago he'd had his mother and he had Christa.

Now he had Thena and Nicky to love and to cherish as well, and he'd never let them go again.

CHAPTER EIGHT

IT WAS impossible to downplay the seriousness of what had just happened. Or how miserably his measures to keep them safe had failed.

Men were waiting for him on the shore—grim-faced men whose instructions had been to protect this pair and they'd missed an obvious threat.

But it hadn't been an obvious threat. This could never be traced to Demos, he thought. This boat had come from nowhere and had gone to nowhere. It could be traced to no one. Even if Thena and Nicky had died today, it would have been written off as a tragedy. A fool in a fast boat...

A fool who'd gone to lengths not to be recognised. A fool with a lethal boat and a gun...

They'd been lucky. So lucky. That these two could swim like fish and that he'd been there...

There was a jetty by the headland at the side of the cove. He took the boat in and the men were ready to catch his mooring lines, to tell him they'd seen the boat coming and tried to radio him but it had been too late, too late.

They were appalled.

He'd thought Demos was capable of anything to get the Crown. No one had really believed him.

Thena hadn't believed him.

She believed him now. Her face said she knew exactly how close she'd come.

'We'll get you up to the palace,' he said gruffly. He put out a hand to help her to her feet.

She didn't take it.

She was trembling. He wanted to take her in his arms and hold her for ever. But she was backing away.

'We're okay,' she said stiffly. 'Nicky, are you okay? Can you walk?'

'Of course I can.' Nicky was recovering more quickly than his mother. Maybe because he hadn't seen the threat for what it really was. 'They were fools,' he said now, indignant. 'They should know not to go so fast near a beach. Can you have them arrested?'

'If they're found,' Nikos said. 'Though I don't have the power to arrest anyone on this island. Your mother can, though.'

She flashed him a look containing a mixture of fear and anger.

'Don't you dare say that. This is it, Nikos. We're going home.'

'The threat will follow you.'

'It won't. We have police in Manhattan.'

'Demos is rich. He can pay…'

'I don't care. I'm not listening. I won't listen.'

'Thena, we'll leave this,' he said softly and he took her hands whether she liked it or not. 'You can't take this in now. Let my men take you up to the palace. I'll meet you there.'

'What are you going to do?'

'I'll contact the authorities on Sappheiros and Khryseis, and on mainland Greece. I'll get out a description of the boat.'

'There are hundreds of pleasure boats like that all along the Greek coast,' one of his men said. 'There's no chance it will be found.'

'I have to try,' he said heavily. 'Thena, please, let my men take you.'

'I will,' she said and tugged Nicky to his feet. 'And then I'm packing. We're leaving for Manhattan tomorrow.'

* * *

He ate a cursory lunch with his mother, and checked on Christa, who was happily drawing pictures of herself and her new brother. He told his mother what he needed her to do, he rang Alexandros, and he set a small army in motion. Then he walked slowly across the headland to the palace.

She had to see sense.

She wasn't in her bedroom. He knocked and when there was no answer he went in. No Thena. He walked across to the adjoining bedroom and twisted the handle.

Dressed simply in jeans and a crisp white blouse, her bare feet tucked up under her, she sat in a big squashy armchair, watching over her sleeping son and her sleeping dog.

She put her finger to her lips, then rose and came out to him, closing the door behind her.

'He was more scared than he'll admit,' she said. 'He heard us talking of Demos. There's a picture of him in the downstairs entrance. Nikos asked if that was the man who was trying to kill us.' She shivered. 'He had a cry, but he's had a bit of lunch and we've talked it out.' She managed a smile. 'He's even talking about what we could do to stop him. And we took down Demos's picture and put it in the trash. So he's okay. But the jet lag's catching up with him as well. I'm glad he's sleeping.'

'You should be sleeping as well,' he said, more roughly than he intended, taking in the shadows under her eyes.

'I can sleep tonight. I won't sleep while Nicky needs me.'

'He's asleep now.' He hesitated. 'Thena, we need to talk.'

'I'm not talking. I'm leaving.'

She was leaning on the closed door. Her hair hadn't been brushed since the swim. She'd obviously showered, tugged on her clothes and that had been enough. There were damp tendrils wisping down her forehead. She obviously didn't care. She was concentrating solely on her son.

Did she have any idea how beautiful she was? Last night in her stunning ball-gown, he'd thought she looked magnificent. But magnificent was too small a word, he thought. He didn't have words to describe how she made him feel.

She was leaning against the door as if she

was protecting the child within. If anything happened to Nicky…

It didn't bear thinking about. He'd thought if anything happened to Christa he'd be gutted. Now he had more to care about. Christa. Thena. And now his son.

There was no way he could let her go back to Manhattan. He wanted her to stay. He wanted to get to know Nicky properly, as a father should.

And…he wanted this woman. Despite their differences, he wanted her.

But there wasn't time to voice his emotions. Wanting Thena had to wait. They had to avert this threat first.

'I want you to go to the Eagle's Nest,' he told her. 'I want us all to go there. You, Nicky, me and Christa.'

She stared at him in incomprehension. 'The Eagle's Nest…'

'Someone in this castle told Demos you were down at the cove,' he said. 'There are people here I'd trust with my life, but the staff is too big for me to know everyone. Thena, I need time to sort things out, and I won't have you at risk while I do.'

'I won't be at risk. I'll have left.'

'You can't leave.'

'I can.'

'Then you'll be watching over your shoulder for the rest of your life.' He met her gaze with strength and unwavering conviction. 'Thena, if anything happens to you and your son, Demos inherits. He and his friends. If you leave then I can't protect you. And, Thena, I *will* protect you.'

'You're saying this because you want Nicky,' she stammered.

'I'm saying it because you're in danger.' Somehow he maintained that flat convincing tone. 'But I won't lie to you,' he said softly. 'I do want Nicky. He needs a father.'

'He's managed just fine without one until now.' But her voice faltered.

How much had she wanted her own father? he wondered. Athena's father had been a weak-willed man who Giorgos had bullied and finally bribed to leave the island almost as soon as Thena was born. As far as he knew, Thena had never seen him.

What would it be like, to be raised not knowing your father? He couldn't imagine. His own father had died when he was twelve but he was still a huge part of who he was. And he had grandparents, cousins, uncles and aunts…a huge extended family to constantly remind him he was loved.

Thena had been brought up by a single mother. Maybe she didn't see the advantages of family.

Maybe he had to teach her.

'So…why are you saying the Eagle's Nest?' She'd obviously been doing her own thinking. Asking about the Eagle's Nest was a concession that it could happen.

The Eagle's Nest was an exquisite castle, built for the sole use of the King. It sat perched high on cliffs overlooking the ocean. One road ran in along winding cliffs that soared as granite buttresses, and the cliffs themselves seemed to become its walls.

'It's safe,' he said.

'Have you been in it?' she asked incredulously. As kids the place had fascinated them.

'I have,' he told her. 'It's fabulous. We should have seen it for the first time together, Thene. We tried hard enough as kids.'

They had. The Eagle's Nest explained two matching broken bones. One sheer rock face rising from the sea. Two kids daring each other…

'We can drive in now like normal people,' he said.

'Right. No one drives into the Nest like normal people.'

'I guess they don't.' He smiled. 'Thena, come on. Come to the Eagle's Nest with me.'

She was refusing to meet his gaze. She was staring along the hall, as if looking for an escape route. 'What...what possible purpose can we achieve by locking ourselves in the Eagle's Nest?'

'It'll give us time,' he said, softly now. 'That's what we need. Alexandros is flying to Athens tonight to try and find Demos. Unfortunately, we believe it's not just Demos behind this. The money at stake... He's weak-willed, there'll be real power trying to get him set up as puppet ruler.'

'I hate this,' she whispered.

'So do I.' He tried to touch her hand but she snatched it away. 'I'd like you to come home with me now and talk to my mother,' he said.

'Your mother?'

He smiled wryly. 'Thena, okay, you don't trust me and why should you? But have you ever had reason to distrust Annia?'

'No, I…'

'Then come. Let her talk to you. Please.'

'She'll talk me into staying.'

'You'll be fearful, whether you go or whether you stay. But if you stay, you'll be safe. We promise you that. Myself. Alexandros. My mother. We'll be your family, Thene.'

'I don't have a family,' she whispered. 'Except Nicky. How can I trust you?'

'You can.'

She stared at him blindly. 'No,' she said at last. 'Not after…' She faltered and then seemed to make a conscious decision to go on. 'Do you know how terrifying it was being pregnant, alone in New York? Do you know how much I depended on you to follow me? How can I trust you, Nikos?'

He grimaced. Christa. Marika. Always the ghost of that long ago nightmare.

But now wasn't the time to talk of the past. He wasn't sure if there ever would be a time, but for now he had to move on.

'What happened in the past is in the past,' he said. 'Maybe we need to remember the time before…before Christa and Nicky were born.

We talked of this when we were kids. We wanted this island to prosper. We both wanted it.'

'That was kids. Dreaming.'

'It might have been, but now we can make it a reality.' He took her hands and held them, whether she willed it or not. But she made no move to withdraw.

'Thena, I believe if you leave the island now, then Demos will win. He'll threaten Nicky, you'll cave in to his demands and he'll end up as Crown Prince. I will not stand by and let that happen.'

'You want to be Crown Prince yourself.'

'I want to change this island,' he admitted. 'I won't lie to you. I want this island to be safe and prosperous. I ache for it. But you've known this. You've known it's who I am.'

'I did think I knew you,' she whispered. 'But Marika…she stopped me knowing you.'

'She was my wife for less than a year.'

'It doesn't matter how long she was your wife. I thought you loved me.'

'I did,' he said softly. 'I always have.' He met her gaze directly, refusing to let her look away. 'I believe I still do.'

'No.' She tugged her hands back. 'Stop it, Nikos. Don't you dare say you love me. I have to leave.'

'You can't leave,' he said steadily. 'Not yet. Okay, forget the emotion. Concentrate on necessity. Thene, this island needs you.'

Maybe he shouldn't be throwing this at her, he thought ruefully, but if she was only part of the Athena he remembered then she'd have to share this love. This passion.

'Look at this palace, Thene—look at it,' he told her. 'It's fabulous and if it was restored…the royal family could use part of it, but what a wonderful public place it would be. Alexandros is doing it on Sappheiros. I want to do it, too.'

'You have it all planned.'

'Not me,' he said. 'Us. We dreamed it, Thene. We walked this island as kids and we wanted it.'

'We were kids.'

'And it was dreams,' he said. 'But Giorgos's death without an heir means those dreams can be a reality. Would you willingly stop them happening by handing over to Demos? Does your career mean so much to you that you'd walk away again? That you'd put Nicky's life at risk in doing so?'

'That's not fair.'

'It's not,' he said steadily. 'Life's not. But this is your second chance. Trust me. Move into the Eagle's Nest until we sort Demos out. Put your career on hold. This time it's not just yourself you're choosing for; it's for your son and it's for the whole island.'

'You think I chose last time?' she whispered.

'When you left…' He frowned. 'Of course you did.'

'I had to go.' She bit her lip and closed her eyes. She was trying desperately to make her muddled mind think.

If he was right…if she really was in danger, and after this morning she had to believe him, then maybe she didn't have the luxury of choice

But to trust him…. There were still so many questions she needed answered.

'So…so where does the money come from?' she asked. 'You came to Manhattan to find me. You obviously paid for these security guards. I know your fishing pays—but does it pay that much?'

He smiled at that. 'It does,' he said. 'I've turned into a businessman. When you have a daughter to care for and there's nothing else to distract you, it's amazing how much energy you can put into a passion. I'm a rich man, Thena. But, even if I wasn't… I'm not in this alone. Alexandros cares for these islands, and so does Stefanos. We'll do whatever it takes to protect our own.'

'Your own being Christa.'

'I meant the islands,' he said, softly now and steadily. 'But yes, Christa, too. I know you feel betrayed by her existence and I'm sorry you feel that way. But I make no apologies for her existence. Nothing gets in the way of what I feel for my daughter. But it doesn't make one speck of difference to what we're planning. It's only… You need to be secure and I need to know my son. Where I go, Christa goes. So we'll make it a family holiday if you like. You, me, Nicky and Christa. Oh, and Oscar bringing up the rear.'

She stared up at him. She should pull her hands away, she thought. She should…she should…

'Nothing gets in the way of what I feel for my daughter.'

That was exactly what she felt for Nicky. No apologies. Nothing. Nicky just…*was.*

She gazed at Nikos and he gazed straight back, unflinching. Strong, direct, secure. Demanding she do what was best for the island. Demanding he get to know Nicky.

Declaring his love for his daughter.

'You should be Crown Prince,' she whispered. 'I've never really belonged here anyway. You've always been the people's prince.'

'You don't give yourself credit,' he said. 'You're the true princess.'

'By an accident of birth. Your mother was a princess. If things had been different, you could have inherited the title.'

'I didn't,' he said flatly. 'I don't want it. Why the hell would I?'

Because it'd keep me safe, she thought. Because it would let me get on with my life.

'It doesn't matter,' she said, suddenly weary. 'Okay. I'll stay. I'll stay until Demos is…I don't know… How can you defuse a threat like that? It might take years. It'll ruin my career.'

'You wanted to write a book.'

'Don't even go there,' she whispered. 'You've just told me I have to sacrifice my job because of this island. Don't trivialise it.'

'I wouldn't, Thene.'

'And don't call me Thene.'

'How can I not?' he said. His hold on her hands tightened. 'Athena, then,' he said softly and smiled. 'I know this isn't what you want but we'll make it work, somehow.'

'You did already,' she said steadily. 'More than you can imagine. But in not telling you about Nicky then I hurt you, too. So let's stick to practicalities. Like drying my hair. And agreeing that we sleep in bedrooms separated by at least two kids. Last night you kissed me…we kissed…and it scared me witless. I lost control and I will not go there again. So I control the locks. If I wish to leave I can at any time. I agree to stay at the Nest for a week and then we'll reconsider. That or nothing.'

'Fine,' he said, and rose. 'I'll go home and tell Annia.'

Her eyes flared in sudden panic.

'Nikos…'

'You're safe,' he told her and, before she knew what he was about, he'd placed his fingers under her chin and kissed her lips. It was a feather kiss, over before it was begun. 'Two of my cousins are at the head of the stairs and they'll stay on guard until we move. I promise you're safe.'

'For how long?'

'If I have my way you'll be safe for ever,' he said, and he said it as a vow. 'What's mine I keep.'

Mine? Was he talking about Nicky? But, before she could respond, he'd kissed her again, harder this time, a kiss to seal a vow.

'I'll be back in a couple of hours to collect you,' he said. 'Me and Christa. But now I need to organise a supply of dog food and a surfboard. How safe does that sound?'

He smiled, then he turned and strode down the hallway, with Athena staring blindly after him.

He'd agreed she could be in control.

She wasn't even close to being in control.

She went back into the bedroom, and she started to shake.

She'd just agreed to move into the royal retreat with Nikos.

Nikos, the sexiest man in the known universe. The people's prince. A fisherman, a business-man. A man who ordered security, who'd saved her life this morning, a man who knew how to protect his own.

She took a couple of deep breaths and tried to steady herself.

Was she overreacting? Maybe she should stop being a drama queen, she told herself. She'd be moving under the umbrella of his protection, for as long as it took to defuse the threat. That was all. Then she'd go back to Manhattan and start her life again.

She looked over to the bed. Her small version of Nikos was still fast asleep.

She wasn't overreacting. The threat this morning had been real and dreadful.

Nikos had saved their son as well.

She closed her eyes—and then suddenly she opened the door again. She flew down the corridor. Down the great marble staircase. Past the two burly fishermen on the stairs. Nikos was already at the grand entrance, striding down to the forecourt.

'Nikos?'

He paused and turned. 'Thene?'

She stopped. He was maybe twelve stairs down from her. She wasn't going any closer.

But she'd run after him for a reason and that reason still held.

'I didn't say thank you,' she said. 'You saved our lives.'

'You saved your own lives by diving.'

'If you and your men hadn't been there...we couldn't have stayed under for ever.'

'Don't think about it,' he said gently. 'Put it behind you.'

'I will,' she said. 'But that doesn't mean...it doesn't mean I don't feel...'

'I don't think we're supposed to feel,' he said dryly. He raised his hand in a mock salute and turned again, striding down the remaining steps two at a time.

And then he stopped. He swung round to face her.

'Hey,' he said suddenly. 'Come with me and see my mother. We need to tell her what we're planning, and you haven't seen her since we got back.'

'I don't think...'

'Don't think,' he said. 'She's not so scary.'

'I know. I...'

'Nicky's asleep. He's likely to stay that way.

My cousins are here watching over him. If you like, you can ask Mrs Lavros to sit with him and phone you the moment he wakes up.' He held out his hand and smiled. 'So Nicky's safe. I promise. And you know my mother would love to see you.'

She looked at his outstretched hand. The urge to take it was almost irresistible.

The urge to trust him was irresistible.

'Why wasn't your mother here last night?' she asked.

'She stayed home and cared for Christa. And she was putting baklava into the oven when I left her this morning.'

Baklava. Nikos's mother's baklava.

'I shouldn't,' she whispered.

'Got you.' He was grinning. 'No one can resist my mother's baklava.'

'For an hour, no more.'

'Excellent,' he said and his hand stayed outstretched.

She walked slowly down the steps towards him. She spent most of the time on the way down staring at that hand.

She shouldn't. She should not.

This was Nikos, taking her to his mother's to

eat baklava as he'd done a thousand times before. The temptation to slip back into that time—that life—was irresistible.

'I'll…I'll talk to Mrs Lavros.'

'Already done,' he said, and called to one of his relatives, who was watching from the top step. 'Joe, can you ask Mrs Lavros to watch over Nicky—ring me the moment he wakes?'

'Consider it done,' the man said and disappeared.

'Are you sure you can you trust Joe?'

'He's my cousin,' he said and grinned. 'My father had eight siblings. Half the islanders are my blood relatives.'

'You should so be the prince here.'

'I don't need to be. Not if you stay.'

And his hand was still outstretched. He was still waiting.

Trust wasn't black and white, she thought. Christa's birth meant that on a personal level she couldn't trust this man. But as guardian of this island…as someone she'd hand over the mantle of rule… Yes, she did trust him.

His hand was still outstretched.

Trust… It was a relative thing. She could trust a little. Just a little. Starting now.

Okay. She would.

She stepped down towards him and put her hand in his and he led the way out of the palace grounds.

He hadn't brought a car so they walked as they'd walked so many times before, along the cliff path leading from the palace to the tiny hamlet where Nikos had lived all his life.

Apart from their disastrous attempt to swim, this was the first time she'd been out of the palace grounds since her arrival. She'd forgotten how beautiful the island was. Or maybe she'd blocked it out, too painful to remember.

It was picture-postcard perfect. Houses clung precariously to the cliff face. The cliffs seemed to be almost stepped down to the sea, with tiny jetties jutting out into the water at their base. Boats swung at anchor; there were a couple tied up at the jetties. Fishermen were tossing their catch to brawny helpers, loading it into trucks for the local market.

'We should be exporting,' Nikos said conversationally as they reached the cliff path. She was so aware of his hand holding hers that she could think of nothing else, but he seemed perfectly at ease. 'This place is alive with fish—we could make a great case for a cannery. As it is, most of the fishermen only catch what the local market can absorb.'

'So what about you?' she managed. She should tug her hand away. But it felt too right. It felt too…good.

'My boats are bigger. We can take our catch directly to the mainland.'

'Which made you independent of Giorgos?' His hold was doing strange things to her. She was slipping into the skin of the girl she had once been—the girl she thought she'd left behind for ever.

'Almost,' he said. 'Though he was always a threat.'

That shook her out of her preoccupation. She knew Giorgos's threats only too well. Should she tell him why she'd left the island all those years ago? Should she share the terror that had made her run?

Why?

If she told him…maybe it would make him feel better about her, but it could never alter what she felt in return.

He was silent beside her. They'd always been able to do this, she thought. Talk when there was a need to talk but otherwise relax with each other so words weren't necessary.

Comfortable in each other's company.

'I do need to get to know Nicky,' he said finally into the silence, as if this was simply an extension of his thoughts. 'You realise he's heir to the throne.'

She hadn't thought this through. 'I guess he is,' she whispered, and the thought of a grown-up Nicky taking control of these islands was almost overwhelming.

Maybe she did need to accept the throne. Maybe she had a duty to make these islands safe—for Nicky.

He should inherit from his father, she thought. And then, she thought, maybe he will. He loves boats. Maybe he'll own a fishing fleet like his father.

Maybe he should grow up here. Maybe it was her duty to keep him here.

There were too many maybes to take in.

They rounded the bend on the headland and Nikos's home was in view. And here was another gut wrench.

Nikos's family home was a cottage, tucked into the cliff tops, surrounded by scores of craypots in various stages of building or repair. Two wooden boats, both decrepit, lay upside down. Tomatoes were growing between the boats and runner beans were climbing over them. A big wooden table lay under straggly olive trees and a couple of faded beach umbrellas were giving shade to hens. It should be a mess—but Athena drew breath with delight.

Home.

And when Nikos opened the back door and ushered her in, the feeling of home became almost overwhelming. The door opened straight into the kitchen. Annia was at the table, her hands covered with flour. She glanced up as Athena entered and gave a cry of delight. Athena was promptly enveloped in a floury hug, as wide as it was sincere.

How long since she'd been hugged like this? She hugged Annia back and felt tears sting behind her eyes.

These were her people. This was her island. How could she have walked away ten years ago and not look back?

She hadn't had a choice. She's known it then and she knew it now. But it felt so good to be here.

'She needs feeding, Mama,' Nikos said. 'Look how skinny she is. How goes it, sweetheart?'

For Christa was at the table. She had a pile of dough and was shaping it into balls.

'I'm cooking,' she told her father proudly. 'You will like my cooking.'

'I will.' He swung her out of her chair, hugged her and set her down again, then straddled a kitchen chair and snagged a taste of whatever was in his mother's mixing bowl.

Athena looked blindly down at him, still fighting tears. Everyone trusted this man. He loved his family. He could never betray them.

How could he have betrayed her so badly?

Something of her emotions must be showing, for Annia was suddenly pulling out a chair and pushing her down.

'You've had a terrifying morning,' she said, peering into her face. 'Word's gone right round the island. That Demos…' She shook her head but she was still looking at Athena. Searching for trouble—and obviously finding it. 'You've had a hard time, my Athena. Ten years of hard time?'

And then she moved straight to the big question. The one Athena had known would be asked. 'And…I have a grandson?' she said tentatively. 'That's what they're saying here. Everyone's saying it. That your son is also Nikos's son. I've asked Nikos and he says I need to ask you. So I'm asking you. Is your Nicky my grandson?'

There was no way she could answer this except with the truth. 'He is,' she said and she didn't look at Nikos. She couldn't.

'Well,' Annia said, and put her floury hands on her hips. Her bosom swelled with indignation. 'You bore my grandson and didn't let us near? You were alone and you didn't tell us? I would have come. In a heartbeat I would have come.'

No, you wouldn't, she thought. You would have been helping Marika with Christa. Two grandchildren within three months. She wanted to yell it at Nikos. Scream it at him.

But Christa was there, happily moulding dough, and neither she or Annia deserved to be hurt.

Annia held a special role on the island—royal but not royal. She was Giorgos's sister. There'd been twenty years' age difference and mutual dislike between brother and sister, she'd married a fisherman and she'd stepped out of the royal limelight, but she still knew more than most what royalty meant to the islanders.

She'd have made a good Crown Princess herself, Athena thought as she sat at the kitchen table she'd sat at so many times before. With her earthy good sense—and with her fabulous son who could have stepped into the role as his right.

'Leave her be, Mama,' Nikos said shortly. 'It's past history. I'm taking Thene and Nicky and Christa…to the Eagle's Nest.'

Annia's face stilled. She looked from Athena to Nikos and back again. And then she smiled.

'To the King's love nest?'

'Mama…'

Her smile was broadening. 'Okay, okay, I'll forget it's other name. So… You're going to the Eagle's Nest—why?'

'To keep Thena safe until we find a way to control Demos.'

Her smile faded for a moment. 'A good idea,' she whispered. 'You'll be safe there.' And then her eyes twinkled into another smile. 'And maybe while you're there you can enjoy it. I was there as a child, with my father, the old King. My Mama showed me their bedroom. It was the closest place to heaven a woman could get, she told me, and it's one of the only regrets I had in marrying your father—that I never got to sleep in that bedroom.'

Then, as Nikos looked bemused, she took Athena's face in her floury hands and kissed her. 'You make sure you enjoy it,' she said. 'And enjoy my oh-so-serious son and make him less serious.'

'I… I'm only staying…'

'Until the island is safe,' Annia finished for her. 'How long is a piece of string?' She smiled. 'You and Nikos… You and Nikos. I suppose the answer to your problems hasn't occurred to you?'

'Mama…' Nikos said again, and his mother kissed him.

'Enough. It's occurred to me—ever since I heard Athena was coming home it's occurred to me. And I'm sure it's occurred to you too, for I'm sure neither of you is stupid. But I will say nothing. So Athena…you want some baklava? It's almost cooked.'

'I…no.'

For she was starting to feel overwhelmed. The domesticity. The gentle, loving teasing. The innuendoes of a relationship with Nikos.

The feeling of being on the outside looking in. She'd hated it all her life and she hated it now.

Once upon a time she'd thought she could find her own place within this circle. It wasn't possible, and Annia's tentative suggestion that she might still was threatening to break her heart.

Annia and Christa—and Nikos—were gazing at her now with various levels of interest and of concern. She didn't want their concern.

She didn't know what she wanted.

Or she did but there was no way in the wide world she'd admit it.

'I need to go back to Nicky,' she said, standing so fast she almost tipped her chair.

Nikos stood and caught it as it fell. 'Problem?'

'I…no. I shouldn't have left him.'

'You know he's not awake yet.' He gestured to the phone on his belt. 'They'd have contacted me.'

'I still need to go.'

'Without baklava?'

'Without anything,' she said and she sounded desperate, she knew, but there wasn't anything she could do about it. It was like claustrophobia, only worse. This kitchen table, this man, this family… They were a dream she'd had since she was eight years old, and twenty years on she wasn't one step closer to achieving it. And now she'd be trapped on this island for heaven knew how long, still on the outside looking in.

She felt sick and sad and empty.

'Thena, don't look like that,' Nikos said, and her eyes flew to his and held. He looked… He looked as if he really cared.

He looked as he'd looked when she'd loved him.

She had to get out of here. Now.

'I'll walk you home,' he said as she backed to the door. Annia and Christa were looking at her with concern and confusion. They might well be confused, she thought. She was so confused she might as well share.

'I'm so sorry,' she whispered to Annia. 'We messed it, Nikos and I. But please…don't hope. Don't tease. It's too late to heal it. You know I should have no right to the throne. My rights are an accident of birth. It's you and Nikos… It should be you and Nikos. I've just got to figure a way around it. Thank you,

Annia. Thank you for everything. And I'm so sorry.'

And she walked out of the cottage before they could say a word. She closed the door and she started to run.

'You should go after her.'

Nikos stared at the closed door and his mother's voice came as if from a long way off. 'She doesn't want me.'

'I think she does.'

He shook his head. 'She left, Mama. Ten years ago she left, and she had my son and didn't tell me. She's strong and independent and willful. And she wants to pursue her career.'

'She doesn't look like a woman whose career is everything.' She hesitated. 'Nikos, can I ask…? Maybe I should have asked this ten years ago. I did think of asking…but I knew it was none of my business. But now… When I see Athena so distressed… You and Marika…' She paused. 'Why did you and Marika marry before a Justice of the Peace and not a priest?'

He frowned. 'Marika was pregnant.'

'Father Antonio would still have married you.'

'Neither of us wanted to be married in the church.'

'I know that,' she said thoughtfully. 'We were upset about it—Marika's mother and I. But you were both adamant. Why were you so adamant?'

'Mama, enough. There are so many arrangements to make…'

'Of course there are,' she said softly. And then she smiled. 'Christa, what is it that you're making?'

'A lady,' Christa said. The dough now had a small blob, a bigger blob underneath, two arms, two legs and what might have been a skirt.

'That's lovely,' Annia said and beamed. 'You make yourself a lady. Nikos, you go and make one safe. And if you can make both of you happy in the process… It's time Father Antonio was put to work.'

CHAPTER NINE

THEY took the limousine again, only this time Nikos was driving. Nicky and Christa were delighted to see each other—far too immersed in the novelty of each other to notice scenery. Athena had her nose against the window the whole way.

She and Nikos had been here before—as kids they'd explored most parts of the island, both on foot and on the back of a saddle-tough pony—but they'd never got past the gates of the Eagle's Nest. The gates were twelve feet high and padlocked, with locks big enough to deter the most intrepid of explorers. Mind, a twelve feet high fence wasn't actually what had stopped them. What had stopped them was the pack of dogs left loose to roam the grounds at will.

'So…um…where are the dogs?' Athena asked nervously as the gates swung open at their approach.

'There was only one left when Giorgos died,' Nikos said over his shoulder. 'The old grounds-man took him home with him. He says he's turned out to be a pussycat. Do you think you can be royal without killer Dobermans?'

'I'll try,' she said magnanimously, and found herself smiling. Despite the trauma of the morning, despite the confusion of her visit to Annia, suddenly there was a frisson of excitement. She felt eight years old again, nose pressed against the twelve foot gate—and suddenly the gate swung open.

'Cool, isn't it?' Nikos said, and it was as if he'd guessed her thoughts. 'The place has always been kept in readiness for a royal visit of up to a dozen guests. So there should be room for us.'

'We'll need four bedrooms,' she said as a knee-jerk reaction. He met her gaze in the rear-vision mirror and grinned. And there it was again. That smile. Pure mischief.

The smile of the Nikos she'd once known…

They drew up before the main entrance. Here again were servants. Two servants.

Joe and Mrs Lavros from the palace.

'I figured we'd go with staff we know,' he told her.

'I can make my own bed and we can make our own sandwiches,' she said, lightness fading. 'Why do we need anyone?'

'I need Joe,' he said flatly.

Once again he met her gaze and the message was unmistakable. Her lightness faded. Joe. Nikos's cousin. Big, burly and totally dependable. Security.

'And Mrs Lavros makes baklava just like Mama does,' he said. 'No aspersions on your cooking, Princess…'

'You think I can't cook?'

'I didn't say that.'

'Mama makes great hamburgers,' Nicky said, leaping to her defence. Then he hesitated. 'One day last winter we made…bak…bakla…what you were just talking about…'

'Let's not go there,' Athena said hurriedly. Nikos grinned—and Nicky grinned with him— and she suddenly had two guys with identical smiles and it was doing her head in.

'So how did your mama's baklava turn out?' he asked.

'We ate it with spoons,' Nicky said, still grinning. 'It was good but it didn't look like the picture in the recipe book. And Mama had to spend half an hour scrubbing honey off the oven.'

'I rest my case,' Nikos said, opening the door of the car. 'Mrs Lavros is here to stay. Okay, kids, it's yours to explore.'

The kids and Oscar tumbled out of the limousine. Mrs Lavros and Joe smiled a welcome and took themselves off, and they were alone on the steps of a fairy tale. Two kids, two adults and one dog. Her family, Athena thought, and then stomped on the thought and concentrated on this truly excellent building.

It was a true fairy tale castle. Built two hundred years ago by a mad monarch with delusions of grandeur, all white stone, turrets and towers, it was like a sugar confection, a magic, secret fantasy.

'Wow,' Nicky breathed, awed. He was standing dumbstruck, staring upwards, seeing a white flag with blue stars and pale yellow stripes fluttering from the battlements. 'What's the flag for?'

'It means the Crown is in residence,' Nikos said.

'The Crown…'

'That would be your mother. Welcome to the Eagle's Nest, Princess.'

'Don't…don't call me that.'

'We don't have a choice,' he said. 'It's time you acknowledged it. This is your place, Princess. You've come home.'

It was fabulous. The more they saw…it was more and more wonderful. The kids whooped through the castle with joy and wonder, and Nikos thought he'd been right to bring them here. He'd been right to include Christa.

The terrors of this morning had faded to nothing for Nicky. He was a kid in a fairy tale castle, he had an adoring little sister at his heels, he had his dog.

He had his mother.

He had his father.

All was right in his little boy's world, and Nikos watched and listened to his excitement and found a peace settling on his heart that had been missing for ten years.

For ten years Thena had been gone. He had his family here—his daughter, his mother, his aunts and uncles and cousins. He'd built his fishing fleet, he'd succeeded on his own terms, he'd almost thought he had enough.

He hadn't. Now, standing by Thena's side as the kids led them on a tour of exploration, he knew his life had suddenly got better.

How to make it complete?

Ten years ago Thena had thought her career was more important than life on this island. He had one more chance to make her see, he thought. To make her understand how wonderful it could be. To see how right it was.

The castle was three storeys high, with the 'Eagle's Nest', a tower with parapets, as the fourth floor. The kids were whooping from room to room on the second floor, choosing bedrooms.

'This one's ace,' Nicky breathed as he discovered a vast bedchamber with a huge four poster bed amid a décor that was pure medieval, right down to a set of armour on either side of the windows. Nicky leaped onto the big bed, Oscar and Christa gamely followed, Nicky tugged the gold tassels holding back the curtains and they were enclosed in a vast velvet tent. The adults were left firmly on the outside.

Oscar shoved his nose out to look at his

mistress, checked she was still there and then dived back to join the kids.

'Can we sleep in here please, Mama?' Nicky breathed from behind the velvet. 'Can we, can we, can we?'

'I guess we can,' she said dubiously. 'It's a pretty big bed. We'll both fit.'

Nicky's head emerged, astonished. 'I didn't mean you, Mama. I meant me and Christa and Oscar.'

'So take that, Mama,' Nikos said at her side, and found himself smiling. For him too, the fears of the morning were dissipating. He should have brought them straight here, he thought. But then…she'd had to go to the palace. She'd had to turn into a princess so she could lay claim to this place.

'I'll sleep next door,' she said, sounding desperate, and both kids launched themselves out from behind their canopy and onto further exploration.

'Don't choose before you've looked at them all,' Nicky ordered, grabbing his mother's hand and tugging her from the room. 'There might be another one as good as this one.'

There wasn't. Not on this floor. Nicky checked

them all and declared them ordinary—bedrooms with French windows and terraces that overlooked the sea, with beds big enough to fit a king and half his courtiers, all were rejected as being not as cool as the one Nicky and Christa had claimed.

'I guess we could share,' Nicky said with magnanimity.

'Nicky, I'll take the one next to yours…'

'There's upstairs,' Nikos said, and Nicky beamed.

'See, Mama, there's upstairs. I like this place. Come on, Christa.'

They were flying upstairs, hand in hand.

Christa had a brother, Nikos thought, stunned, and glanced at Thena and saw she was as stunned as he was.

'I thought this might take years,' he said.

'I didn't… I can't…'

'Though maybe they're like us,' he said. 'We met when we were eight years old and we knew right then that we were going to be best friends. Friends for ever.'

'Don't…'

'We were, Thene,' he said softly. 'We still could be. Surely your career can be redirected.

I don't mean give it up entirely. But you've given so much for it already…'

'Don't,' she said again and she was close to tears.

He wouldn't push. He mustn't. He had her here. He had time.

And then there was a whoop of absolute joy from above their heads.

'We've found your bedroom. Come on up. Mama, Papa, come on up.'

Mama, Papa… Nicky had shouted the words as naturally as breathing. *Mama, Papa…*

It took their breath away.

'Shall we go take a look?' Nikos said and put his hand out to her.

She took a deep breath. She stared down at his hand.

And then, deliberately, she put her hands behind her back and walked up the stairs.

There was still so much between them. How did you learn to trust again? No matter how desperately you wanted to…how did you take that leap?

But then she reached the top of the stairs and

the door to the third floor bedroom, and she stopped thinking of anything else.

The third storey was part of the tower, narrowing to the nest itself on the fourth floor. The top of the tower was a circular fortification on top of the building where one looked over the parapets to see the entire island. Or that was what she'd imagined. She'd just never imagined what lay beneath.

All her childhood she'd seen this part of the castle—a stark white tower seemingly growing from the crags of the northern highlands. The tower could be seen from all over the island, from out at sea, maybe even from the far islands of Sappheiros and Khryseis.

It was almost dusk. The islands, all white stone cliffs and blue-green mountains, glittered like jewels reflecting the tangerine rays of the setting sun. The sea stretched out in every direction, reflecting the sunset. Below them were fishing boats, heading for harbour, heading for home.

She could see everything, because, apart from the tiny vestibule allowing access, there was nothing between them and a three hundred and sixty degree view of sea and sky.

She was on top of the world.

There were no lights, she saw. Instead there were candles. Hundreds of candles, set into wall embrasures. But they weren't lit yet—they didn't need to be. The setting sun gave a tangerine glow to the whole world.

Beneath her feet the carpet was lush and deep, but apart from the view the focus of the room was the bed. How had they ever got it up here? It must have been built on site.

It was a full circle, a great island in the centre of the room. As big as two king-sized beds, it was made up with vast antique quilts of deep crimson and lovely faded silver. The silver and the crimson were caught up in cushions, hundreds of cushions, soft, squishy. Nicky had already picked up an armload and was tossing them indiscriminately at Christa and at Oscar.

Christa was giggling and tentatively tossing a cushion back.

But then Nicky realised Nikos and Athena were at the door, staring in with stunned amazement. 'Look at the sky,' he demanded and grabbed Christa's hand, and they clambered onto the great bed, lay on their backs and gazed upward.

Thena gazed up as well.

And gasped.

The ceiling was a vast glass dome, sweeping upward as part of the great central tower. It was one enormous window, built of hundreds and hundreds of lead framed glass panels forming one magnificent window to the sky.

The setting sun was glittering in from the windows so Athena's attention had been distracted to the lower level. But now… She gazed up in awe at a vast expanse of sky, the soft scudding clouds of sunset and the first hint of the evening star.

'This is so cool,' Nicky breathed. 'It hasn't got a tent like our bedroom but it's cool anyway. It's like flying.'

She could see the simile. In this room she was on top of the world. She was almost floating.

'Will you and Papa sleep in here?' Nicky demanded and she came down to earth fast.

'I…no. I'll sleep next to your bedroom.'

'It's okay, Mama,' Nicky said magnanimously. 'Christa and Oscar and I don't mind if you sleep up here. I won't be scared if I have Christa. And you won't be scared if you have Papa.'

Papa. The word was part of his vocabulary already.

That was enough to choke her right up, to make her world twist from its axis. Nicky had a papa.

She glanced at Nikos and his eyes were hooded and enigmatic. But she knew this man. She knew this expression. It meant he was struggling hard not to show emotion.

He wanted his son. He was falling in love with her Nicky.

Her son had a father.

Her son was telling her she had to sleep with Nikos.

'Nikos and I don't share a bedroom,' she said, too curtly.

'Why not?' Both the children were gazing at them now. They'd found this room for them. For a moment Athena thought they'd taken it personally if she didn't accept their find as a delight.

'Thena can sleep in here,' Nikos said, and his voice was as guarded as his expression. 'She probably snores. Grown ups snore a lot. If you guys don't mind, I'll sleep down in one of the downstairs bedrooms so her snores don't drive me crazy.'

'I don't think she snores,' Nicky said doubtfully.

'She has the look of a snorer.'

'Hey.' She was torn between laughter and tears. Laughter was by far the preferred option but tears were certainly close.

'What do snorers look like?' Nicky asked.

'They have fat noses,' Nikos said and looked up to the windows and stroked his own nose. 'As opposed to you and me, Nicky. We have the Andreadis nose. Thin, straight and exceedingly handsome.'

'I do not have a fat nose,' Athena exclaimed.

'Snub, I'd say,' Nikos said indulgently. 'Cute, but definitely not aristocratic.'

The conversation had suddenly veered away from snoring—away from bedrooms—which was definitely a relief.

'I have your nose?' Nicky was supremely unaware of the emotional undercurrents running between the adults. He was concentrating on himself, and on Nikos, and on this new relationship which he'd hardly had a chance to explore. 'And I have your cowlick. And I don't get seasick.'

'So you're a true Andreadis.'

'But I'm Nicholas Christou.'

'Christou's your mother's name,' Nikos said. 'If I'd married your mother you'd be an Andreadis.'

'I like being a Christou.'

'I expect you do,' Nikos said easily but Athena's mind had taken off again.

Christa... Christou...

She was Athena Christou. Something occurred to her which hadn't had time to surface until now. But it hit her then. How had Marika felt about her daughter being named so closely after Nikos's ex-girlfriend?

Maybe neither of them had ever thought of it. Maybe Marika had never seen her as a threat.

It was so long ago. Why did it still have the capacity to sting now?

'So what do we do now?' Nicky said, moving on.

'Supper and bed?' Nikos suggested and Nicky's face fell. So did Christa's. She'd been gamely following the conversation and she got this.

'Play,' she said very firmly, and Oscar wagged his tail in agreement.

Athena almost groaned. She was so tired she could hardly stand. The emotional strain of the last twenty-four hours was added to sheer physical fatigue. But, of course, Nicky had slept this afternoon and he hadn't spent last night dancing. He was raring to go.

'Tell you what,' Nikos said, and he glanced at Athena with that careful, assessing look she was starting to know. And to fear? The look that said he knew what she was thinking. 'How about we have a light supper and then I take Christa and Nicky down to the beach for a swim before bed?'

'Is it safe?' she demanded before she could stop herself and then could have kicked herself. For Nicky's face registered alarm, and he moved fast to stand beside her.

And Nikos got that, too. 'You needn't worry,' he said, gently but firmly. 'Nicky, what happened this morning will not happen again. We have lookouts now, watching the island's waters. And under this castle, down a secret little path known only to us, there's a tiny cove, rimmed by reefs. The water inside the reef is calm and clear and is only just deep enough for swimming. It's full to the brim with fish—no one's ever been allowed to swim here and the fish show no fear. No boat can get over the reef to reach here. Do you trust me enough to take you there without your mother?'

And it wasn't up to her. It was Nicky himself who decided.

'Yes,' he said, firmly and surely, and he moved confidently away from her side. 'We trust Papa, don't we, Mama?'

'I...yes,' she faltered and was saved from having to say anything more by the whoop of delight as Nicky took her yes to mean not only that she trusted in Nikos, but also that it was okay to swim after dinner. Without her.

It seemed Nicky was now a part of Nikos's family, whether she belonged or not.

The kids went whooping out of the bedroom, up the last remaining flight of stairs to the parapets that capped the tower. Nikos stayed back. There weren't words to express what either of them were feeling. Or maybe neither of them knew what they were feeling.

There were things to be said but neither of them knew where to start.

Finally he stood aside to allow her to precede him from the room.

'He's safe with me, Thene,' he said softly as

she passed him, and she thought, yes, I know he is.

Her son was part of Nikos's family.

And she…she was jealous.

CHAPTER TEN

THEY had supper informally in the ancient kitchen at the back of the castle. It was big enough to feed a small army, Athena thought, but it was still…good. The ancient flagstones, the vast old range sending its gentle heat across the room, the scrubbed copper pans hanging from hooks, lavender hanging in bunches from the beams, windows open to let the sounds of the sea drift in, bird feeders hung in the windows…

'This castle doesn't look as if it's been deserted for years,' she said, puzzled, and Mrs Lavros nodded.

'It hasn't. Though Giorgos didn't come here we've loved it. As we've loved the palace. We always knew you'd come home.'

'And now you have,' Nikos said gently and

raised his glass to hers. 'Here's to you, our Princess Athena. Long may she reign over us.'

'I'm not… I can't…' She caught her breath in panic. What was he saying? 'We'll be going back to the States…'

'Not yet, Mama,' Nicky said, and he sounded… scared.

As well he might, Thena thought frantically. Her little boy was frightened of leaving this island now. The only safe place for him was…by Nikos's side.

She glanced up and found Nikos's gaze on her, thoughtful, maybe even stern.

'You can't leave, Thena.'

What was she supposed to say to that? She couldn't think of a thing.

'I'm…I'm tired,' she managed. 'If…if you don't mind, thank you, Mrs Lavros, that was lovely, but I'm really tired. Nicky, when you come back from the swim come and tell me about it.'

'You'll be asleep,' Nikos said, teasing.

'I won't be asleep until I've made sure Nicky is safe,' she said and suddenly she inexplicably felt like weeping. It was so hard. It was so, so hard.

Long may she reign over us?

That sounded awfully lonely from where she was sitting.

She didn't sleep. Lying on the huge bed, looking up at the vast expanse of sky, it was as if she'd forgotten who she really was. She was nothing. Insignificant and lost. If she was confused before, she was even more confused now.

That was bad enough—but how could she sleep when Nikos…when the children were playing on the beach right underneath her windows? She got up and walked over to the window. Floodlights set up on the cliff face meant the sheltered little cove was as safe as in daytime. There were lights out on the water as well, tiny buoys floating on the swell. The bigger surf was caught and contained by the circular reef so the waves within were gentle, the light-buoys floating up and down in synchronisation with the gentle waves.

Christa had a rubber surf mat. She was holding on tight, floating in the shallows, giggling, watching her papa teach Nicky to surf. Nikos had produced his surfboard and was already teaching Nicky to catch the waves.

'When it comes you need to be paddling almost as fast as the wave,' Nikos was saying and a trick of sound made his voice carry all the way up to where she stood. 'Okay, here comes a good one. Paddle, paddle, go!'

The wave caught him, and Nicky hung on for dear life as the wave carried him all the way to the sand.

He stood up, exultant, in the shallows. Big with excitement. 'I caught it. I caught it!'

'We'll have you kneeling on the board by tomorrow,' Nikos said. 'And standing by the end of the week.'

But she'd heard enough.

She turned away and walked back to the too big bed, lay down and stared up at herself. Multiplied by plenty.

'Nicky needs his papa,' she told Jupiter—or was it Venus? 'He should stay here.

'You need his papa.' Right. She was talking to a planet.

It was probably a star, she told herself. Surely it was okay to discuss the meaning of life with a star.

'To stay, I'd have to trust him,' she told…what the heck, Venus.

'I think I do trust him.'

But she—or Venus—was lying.

She might not trust him—but she loved him.

That was the only truth. She'd given her heart away when she was eight years old and she'd never taken it back. But that one dreadful betrayal… It didn't mean she loved him less. It was as if there was some part of her that had got it wrong. She'd trusted him so absolutely that his betrayal had destroyed a part of herself.

She hugged herself and Venus tucked herself behind a cloud in sympathy.

There were still a thousand stars. All wanting to talk to her.

She was never going to sleep in this room.

Where, then? On the same floor as Nikos and the children?

'They're together. I'm on my own,' she whispered and then thought, ooh, who's feeling sorry for herself?

There was a shout of laughter from down in the cove. She climbed out of bed—it was almost a marathon to get to the side—and walked back out on the balcony.

They were playing Falafel.

It was a game she and Nikos had played as kids.

When Annia made falafels she formed her little balls of chickpeas and parsley into balls and then rolled them in flour until they were thoroughly coated.

So Athena and Nikos would swim until they were wrinkly as prunes, then race up the beach and roll and roll in the dry sand until every inch of them was coated. Then run round being falafels. They were doing it now—two kids and Nikos. Two kids and their papa.

Completely coated in dry sand, they stood— then Nikos spread his arms and moaned like a great sandy spectre and started chasing them.

The children squealed in delight. The beach at dusk…she'd always thought it was the most magical of times, and here was her son, learning about it for himself. With his papa.

Nicky ran and ran. Christa was far easier to catch but Nikos made it seem as if it was just as hard to catch her. Finally he had them, a child under each arm, and was staggering back to the water to wash them off. Oscar brought up the rear, barking his delight.

And suddenly she was crying.

Damn, she was crying.

Nikos looked up from the beach. And saw her.

He stilled. At his feet the children whooped and splashed in the shallows. But Nikos simply stood—and watched.

And, from nowhere, into her heart came the words he'd used so often.

Dare you.

Dare she take a chance? Dare she forget what had happened ten years ago?

Dare she move forward?

It was too soon. It was too fast.

She had to get rid of these stupid, wussy tears.

She turned and started to go inside.

'Thena!' It was a call from the beach, strong and demanding. She should ignore it. She should…

She turned.

He was still watching her.

'Dare you,' he called, and she gave a gasp of fright. What was it about this man? How did he know what was inside her head?

Did he know that she loved him?

She turned and headed back to her bed and her stars and her confusion.

If she talked to a thousand stars she might just get some answers.

Or not.

She'd left him for a career.

She'd had a career. She'd succeeded on her terms. Surely enough was enough. Surely he could convince her to stay.

He stood in the shallows and watched her back away from the balcony, head indoors and haul the French windows closed after her.

He'd swear she was crying.

'Does your mama cry much?' he asked Nicky conversationally, as if this was a guy to guy discussion of the female sex.

'Only when she thinks I'm asleep,' Nicky told him.

'So she cries at night?'

'I'm not supposed to know,' Nicky said. 'But sometimes when I snuggle into bed with her in the morning her pillow's soggy.'

'Why do you think she gets sad at night?'

'I used to think it was 'cos she was lonely,' Nicky said. 'But she's got me and she's got Oscar. Only now I know about here...' He stood and gazed around him, a small boy taking in a small boy's heaven. 'Now I think it must be 'cos she was lonely for you.'

'For…for this island, you mean?'

'Mama says things and places don't matter,' Nicky said. 'She says only people matter. So I figure it's you.'

He brought the children up from the cove. Mrs Lavros helped bath them and get them to bed. Athena didn't appear. Nikos half expected Nicky to want his mother, but they discussed it and decided if she hadn't wanted to swim she must be very tired indeed. So Nicky himself decided if he was sleeping with Christa and with Oscar there was no need to disturb her.

So Nikos sat beside their tent-cum-bed and started to read them a story—only Nicky objected.

'I have a book in my bag,' he told Nikos. 'It's really good. Mama lets me read to her. Can I read it to you? Is that okay?'

'Sure,' Nikos said, so he sat and watched as his son read his daughter a bedtime story and it was hard not to tear up himself.

It was Thena who wept, he told himself. Real men don't weep.

What was the concept of a real man?

His father had been a real man. He'd died of a heart attack when Nikos was twelve, and Nikos had adored him.

His father had loved Nikos and had been totally, unconditionally proud of him. Even though he'd been dead for many years, that love lingered on. As did the echoes of his care.

'Anything happens to me, you care for your mother, Nikos. She's the light of my life. You and your mother... You're my whole heart.'

A real man had a family and loved them unashamedly. A real man would face any terror to keep that family safe.

His parents had had disagreements—loud disagreements—but they'd never frightened him. Because they'd always ended in exasperated laughter, in hugs, in his father saying, 'Your mother is impossible—an impossible woman—how am I to live with such a woman?'—and then cooking his biggest lobster and opening a bottle of wine and playing music his mother didn't like, too loud.

And his parents dancing and him watching in

sleepy contentment until they put him to bed and had the night for each other.

So…so what?

What was between him and Thena…it was a disagreement so enormous that no lobster would be big enough.

But to let that betrayal eat away at them for ever…

Maybe his father would say: 'So what if Thena left you ten years ago? So what if she didn't tell you she had your son? You know your actions must have distressed her unutterably, too.'

He couldn't defend his actions. Was it fair therefore to ask her to defend hers?

What if he could simply say that was past history? Move on.

Move onto family.

To two children. A dog.

To a wife?

Ten years ago he'd asked her to marry him and she'd wept with joy. But things had changed. She no longer trusted him. If he was to ask her to marry him now…she'd assume it was because of the Crown, that he wanted control.

And maybe he did. If he married her he could keep her safe. It would stop Demos in his tracks. He'd be royal himself.

How could he ask her to marry him?

Christa was already fast asleep. Nicky read on, but his voice was starting to stumble. He lifted the book from Nicky's hands, tucked him under the covers and then thought why not? And he kissed his son goodnight.

Such a little thing—but not small at all. Huge.

How could he ask Thena to marry him?

Dare you?

He left the bedroom and closed the door gently behind him. He turned, and Thena was watching him from the shadows.

He stilled. 'Hi,' he said cautiously.

'Hi, yourself.'

'I thought you were asleep.'

She was ready for bed. She was in a pale blue wrap, floor-length. Bare toes, though. Her curls were a tangle—had she been trying to sleep?

'How can I sleep when I keep thinking of you?' she murmured.

'That'd give anyone nightmares.'

She tried to smile but her smile didn't reach her eyes. 'Nikos…'

'Come up to the tower,' he said and put his hand out to take hers. She looked down at his hand—appeared to think about it—and then placed her hand in his.

A tiny step… Why it made his heard thud…

It did. His heart definitely thudded. Whoa, he was in trouble here.

Dare you?

He led her up the stairs. On the landing that led to her bedroom he swiftly led her past. It was a bit too soon to face that room.

The stairs grew narrower the higher they climbed. The tower was just that, an eyrie built for a birds-eye view of the whole island. The tower narrowed the higher they climbed, so he was forced to fall behind.

He'd read somewhere—where was it?—that gentlemen always followed their ladies upstairs and preceded them down so they could catch them either way.

Their hands were still loosely linked—she didn't seem to want to pull away and he'd have rather died—but what he really wanted to do was pick her up and carry her.

She was climbing before him, in her lovely soft robe, her bare feet on the cold stones—if he carried her, then her feet wouldn't get cold.

But he was aware he was holding his breath. There were so many questions that needed answers, and he thought many of those questions were to be resolved in the next few moments.

He mustn't push too fast. Picking her up and carrying her might panic her and that was the last thing he intended.

And then they were at the top—a circular walk, built as battlements around the central dome. He didn't want to think about the dome. The ceiling to Thena's bedroom. *Thena's.*

All around them stretched the warm Mediterranean night. A great moon hung low on the eastern sky, climbing ponderously upward to join the star-filled heavens. The great galaxy of the Milky Way spread above them, stars beyond and beyond and beyond.

'We used to try and count them,' Nikos said softly, and her hand tightened in his.

'It used to scare me—made me feel so small.'

'And do you feel so small now?'

'Smaller,' she whispered. She was leaning back against him as she gazed out in wonder.

To the west was Sappheiros, the largest of the Diamond Isles. North was Khryseis. The lights from the Far Isles glittered through the night, mysterious and beckoning. Closer to home, they could see the lights of boats, riding at anchor; the tiny lights from cottages spread among the mountains; and in the distance the far-off lights of the royal palace. Her royal home?

'This is yours, Thena,' he whispered softly into her hair. 'It's yours to rule as you will. We always dreamed it would come to you, and now it has. You can't walk away from it now. It's your birth-right, your heritage…'

'My duty,' she whispered back, and he thought he heard the first faint trace of acceptance. 'Nikos, I can't do this alone.'

'You won't have to, Princess. I'll be beside you every step of the way. If you can put your career on hold… I know it's so important to you…'

'My career is not important.'

For a moment he thought he hadn't heard right. She was leaning into him, her spine curving against his chest, her dark curls just brushing his chin. She was the loveliest creature. His Thena.

But he had to think past her body. He had to think past what her touch was doing to him.

'You mean…your career isn't important any more?' he asked cautiously.

'It never was.' And then, reluctantly it seemed, she pulled away from his grasp. She turned and leaned on the parapet, as if she needed to see him to make him understand what she wanted to say.

'Don't get me wrong; I always wanted to be a writer,' she said, and he knew she was struggling against the emotion of the moment to make her voice prosaic. 'I always did and maybe I always will. When I was twelve I wanted to be a cutting edge crime reporter. Then I wanted to be a poet. By the time my mother died I wanted to write a history of this island, an exposé of Giorgos's corruption. I wanted to use my writing to save the world. But then…'

'But then you were offered a cadetship on a fashion magazine in New York.'

'No,' she said, tightly now, as if it was desperately important. 'I was given the cadetship. It was paid for. I was told it had been arranged that I start work in Manhattan in two weeks. I was told my accommodation was paid for. I was given a one way airline ticket and enough money to keep me for a year. and I was told to get off the island and never come back.'

He stared at her. Disbelieving. All the breath seemed to have been sucked from his body. 'By?' But he didn't need to ask.

'By Giorgos, of course,' she said.

'But you didn't have to take it.'

'You think?'

'You could have refused.'

She shook her head. She closed her eyes as if remembering a nightmare and opening her eyes on it would start the horror all over again.

'You were just starting to succeed,' she whispered. 'Since your papa died you'd worked so hard to make your boat support you and your mother. And you were starting to make it prosper. That's what Giorgos was afraid of. You were the son of his sister—a royal from his own line. You were starting to make serious money. And you'd just asked me to marry you. If I married the King's sister's child, there'd be

royalty on both sides; two people the locals knew
and trusted. Giorgos feared the islanders would
rebel. He said I had to follow his orders or he'd
dynamite every boat in the harbour and he didn't
care much if anyone was on them. And he'd run
you and your mother off the island. He said the
only way I could prevent that happening was by
leaving. So…so I left.'

'Thena…' He moved towards her but her
hands were out, as if to fend him off.

'No. There's no use being angry. There's no
use being anything.'

'If you'd told me…'

'You would have…done something stupid,'
she whispered. 'My hero. My Nikos. I knew…or
I thought I knew…that your fury on my behalf
would know no bounds. I was afraid of him, I
was afraid for you and I was afraid for your
mother. So I left. I…I hoped you'd follow. That
was dumb. Obviously, there were…things that
prevented you leaving. So I started work in New
York. A couple of months later I realised I was
pregnant. I was lucky enough to find a wonderful landlady. I worked right up until Nicky was
born, and when he was two months old I went

back. I've worked ever since. So…' She took a deep breath. 'So, yes, I'm proud of my career. I'm proud I supported myself and Nicky. I've even enjoyed a lot of it. But don't say I sacrificed everything for my career. Don't say it, Nikos. Because it's just not true and tonight…tonight I want the past to be over. I want to put history behind us. I want to move on.'

'Thena…' It was a groan of pain.

He didn't know where to go from here. He couldn't think. What she'd gone through. And she'd acted out of love, for him, for everyone.

'Don't,' she said and took his head in both her hands and tugged him forward. 'What's done is done. I can't bear to think of ten years ago. I don't want to think of it and why should I? All I know is that you've come back into my life again. Am I misreading the signs, Nikos, as I misread so badly before? Is it you in there? The Nikos I thought I knew? The Nikos who dared to love me?'

'Who dared…'

'Who dared,' she whispered. 'When all the rest of the island avoided me for fear of Giorgos, you dared to be my friend. And then you dared to love me. I don't know what happened after that. I don't want to know. All I know is that I'm home now, exactly where I want to be, and I'm with the man I want more than anything in the world.' She hesitated. 'And I'm trying really hard not to be forward here, but if you don't kiss me I'll very likely explode, or die of humiliation, or…'

Or he'd never know. Because enough was enough. He had her in his arms and he was tugging her close with ruthless strength. She was yielding, her lips were meeting his, her hands were tugging him close, closer, deepening the kiss so the night disappeared, melting into the star-filled sky, transforming with a wonder he thought he'd lost and was now magically his again.

Thena. His Thena. Trusting as she'd trusted once before. Weighing up the sorrow, the hurt he knew he'd caused her with the birth of Christa, with his marriage to Marika, and moving on.

Forgiving…even when she didn't know the truth.

He loved her so much.

He pulled back a little so he could read her

face. And what he saw there made his heart twist within him.

She was looking at him as if she loved him.

She loved him. She must love him. That one betrayal had been an aberration—not her Nikos. The Nikos she'd known then could never have done such a thing.

And, even if he had, the Nikos kissing her now could surely never repeat such a betrayal.

But right here, right now, she no longer cared. Nikos was right here, right now, his eyes dark and fathomless, waiting for her to say what she needed to say—if she could ever figure out what that was.

Okay, say it, she told herself. Just say it.

'So…so this is the most romantic place in the Eagle's Nest?' she managed.

'It's not,' he said, fast and sure. 'It's a place of stone and parapet and view—which is all very well if you want stone and parapet and view, but if you want more…'

'If I want more?'

His dark eyes flashed with something she wasn't sure of. Surprise? Laughter? No. Something much, much deeper.

'I'd surely give it,' he said softly. 'But I've hurt you so badly in the past.'

'You have.'

Years ago she'd fallen in love with this man. He'd betrayed that love in the worst possible way, but she'd moved on, she'd grown up and she'd got herself a life. She'd become independent of both Nikos and his island.

But now… She wanted to trust as she'd trusted so long ago. Innocence regained.

Stupid concept, but…

'You think we could maybe learn to trust each other?' Nikos asked, and it was as if he was following her thoughts.

'After so long?'

'You bore my son,' he said steadily. 'You had him alone and I can't begin to imagine how that must have been for you. I can't bear to think that you couldn't contact me—that you couldn't tell me of his existence. But now…I'm finding there are more things I can't bear. Like the thought of you leaving. Once you dreamed of writing freelance. Is there any way you could do that here?'

'So…so you'll have more time with Nicky?'

He placed his hands on her shoulders and he looked at her as if he could read behind her eyes.

'I do want my son,' he said, softly but surely. As if it was a vow. 'Nicky *is* my son and from now on I intend to be a father to him, in any way I can. I want him—but I want you, too. Thena, if I'd known… If I'd guessed…'

'It doesn't matter.' It did, but not tonight. Tonight was hers. Tonight was her dream time, history had never happened and she was surrendering herself to the here and now.

As was Nikos.

'I believe ten years ago is best forgotten,' he whispered, tugging her close, folding her against him and wrapping her in his arms. 'For tonight, at least.'

And then he kissed her, long and hard, as she'd ached to be kissed for ten long years, as she longed to be kissed for ever.

Ten years dissipated just like that. He was her Nikos. Hers! And she was his, with every fibre of her being.

When the kiss ended they both knew it was immutable truth.

'Will you come to my bed, my love?' he asked,

in a voice that sounded shaken. And then the loved laughter returned. 'Or…your bed?'

'Aren't there enough stars out here?'

'Not for the serious gazer,' he told her, and the wicked laughter was back. Gloriously back.

'Counting stars beats counting sheep. That is, if we can't think of anything else to do.'

She had to be serious here. Laughter would not do.

'Last time we did what I understand you're suggesting, I believe we made Nicky,' she said in a voice that was none too steady.

'So we're older and wiser—and a bit more prepared.'

'You're prepared?'

'I believe I am.' He was tugging her close again, kissing her eyelids, each in turn.

'So am I,' she whispered.

The kissing stopped. She was held at arm's length again. Nikos's face showed blank astonishment. 'Did I just hear what I thought I heard?'

'I might be forgetting most of the last ten years,' she said, beginning to laugh. 'But there are a couple of things I need to remember. Like the lecture given to me by my doctor after

Nicky's birth. If you think I'd come within a hundred miles of you again without contraception, you're not the man I think you are, Nikos Andreadis.'

'My Thena!' And the laughter was back. The wonderful laughter that had blazed between them since the hour they'd first met.

'Don't you dare laugh,' she said, but she couldn't help herself. She was laughing as well, at his laughter, at his joy, at the assurance of joy to come.

At the knowledge that for this night this man was hers. He always had been, she thought, from the time she'd met him to now. She'd borne his son. She'd carried him in her heart for ever.

'I'm not laughing,' he told her and it was true. The laughter had changed. He was watching her now with eyes as dark as night, with an expression on his face she'd never seen before—of tenderness, of joy, and of something more.

Of hope for the future?

That was what it was, she thought as she melted into him, as he lifted her into his arms and carried her unprotesting down the winding staircase, to a vast bedchamber with windows looking out in every direction to the sea beneath and to the islands beyond. As he laid her tenderly on the bed—a bed big enough for a king or six, piled high with feather pillows so soft she almost disappeared into them. As he pulled the curtains, one after another, cutting out the view, the islands, the sea, the outside world. Everything but the sky.

As he lit the candles, one by one.

And as he came to her where she lay, waiting for the man of her dreams.

He unfastened his shirt and she watched him, awed, fascinated, so deeply in love she thought she could die right now and be happy.

She matched him button for button, unfastening her robe. His dark eyes flared with passion. His shirt was gone long before she had her robe undone—why weren't her fingers working?—but it didn't matter. For he was helping her.

And finally she was free. His hands slipped in beneath her nightgown to cup her breasts and she wanted to cry out with sheer happiness. Sheer joy.

She was pushing her nightgown down, desperate to be closer. He helped her, kissing as he went, touching, tasting, loving, until her body was flames.

Nikos. Her first and last love. Nikos…

She was naked, gloriously, wonderfully naked, and so was he. He was sinking into the pillows beside her, gathering her into his arms.

His body was against her body. Skin against skin—the most erotic sensation in the world.

The heartbreak of years faded to nothing. The children, the island, responsibilities—everything was gone.

There was only this man, this love and this night.

There was only Nikos.

She woke and the world she'd lived in for ten long years had disappeared.

This was a fantasy—a fairy tale. At some time in the future it would end, but for now she was selfish enough, needy enough, to say thank you very much, this is where I belong. Maybe when reality hits I'll have a long time to remember this, so I need to soak up every precious moment.

She was lying in the arms of the man she loved with all her heart. And, whether she believed it or not—and yes, her head was screaming at her to be wary—the feeling seemed to be reciprocated. Nikos was loving her as he'd loved her ten years ago. But this was a grown man now, a businessman, a prince of the people, a lover, a man with strength and gentleness, laughter and tenderness, wonder and hope.

He was hers and she was his. For now they were two lovers exulting in each other's bodies. Drowning in each other's eyes.

And the place where they were loving was over-the-top fantastic.

'I'm hoping this glass is one way,' Nikos murmured in the aftermath of loving. 'Otherwise we could have some very shocked seagulls. You think we should declare this place a fly free zone?'

'And enforce it how?'

'I can't,' he said morosely. 'I believe it's you who's in charge of royal decrees.'

She giggled.

But then… Her giggle was echoed from outside the door. Two giggles.

'Uh-oh,' Nikos said. Athena dived under the covers and Nikos had his pants on and was fastening his shirt before three small faces appeared around the door. Two kids and a dog. Oscar took one look and leaped with joyous abandon onto

the bed, and Nicky and Christa landed straight
after. Athena was overwhelmed by dog and kids.
Nicky hugged her, Christa hugged her too, on the
basis of what was good for Nicky was okay by
her, and Oscar licked every face in reach.

Her family. She was buried in family. She
hugged and sniffed and she glanced up and saw
her emotions reflected on Nikos's face.

No. Not her family.

Their family.

'Did you both sleep in here?' Nicky demanded,
awed.

'I'm happy to tell you your mother didn't
snore—very much,' Nikos said magnanimously.
'I slept on this side of the bed, she slept on the
other and if I piled the pillows really high it was
just a muted little snortle.'

'Ooh,' Athena said, and emerged from kids
and dog long enough to toss a pillow at him. Her
aim wasn't bad considering the handicap she
was under—clutching bedclothes so the kids
wouldn't discover she was naked. But Nikos
hadn't defended himself and he was thumped
right in the chest.

'Yay,' Nicky said and took his lead from his

mother, and in seconds pillows were going every-where.

Her family.

Their family.

Betrayal was a thing of the past, she thought mistily, giggling and tossing the odd pillow herself. Now was just for…now.

They had three days and three nights of magic.

Athena asked no questions. She was simply living in the moment. Nikos watched her as the days wore on and thought she was holding the kids to her, holding him to her, as if she feared they could be snatched away at any moment.

Somewhere outside the castle Demos was still plotting. Nikos was sure of it. But Alexandros was working on his behalf. Nikos's job was to keep his little family here; keep them safe until the threat could be defused.

It was no hardship at all. It was pure magic.

He had his kids. He had Thena. As far as he was concerned Alexandros could take as long as he needed to defuse the threat. This time out was theirs.

* * *

244   BETROTHED: TO THE PEOPLE'S PRINCE

Only of course reality finally had to intrude.

Nikos had organised the lawyers to come on the third day.

'We need to get things settled before we go back to the palace,' he told her.

'Um…aren't things settled?'

'The affairs of the island aren't,' he said, kissing her on the nose. 'So tomorrow it's lawyers.' Then he hesitated. 'Thene, it's going to be a long, boring day. My mother is asking if she could take Nicky and Christa. They'll be safe—Demos can gain nothing by hurting one of you alone, and I'll send Joe with them to make sure. Do you think Nicky would like to go?'

'We'll ask him,' she said, and did, and Nicky thought the idea of a grandmother was too cool for words.

When Annia came to fetch them in an ancient Land Rover with no roof, he decided she was even cooler. They piled into the back seat, only to discover one of Annia's hens had decided this was a great nesting box. So off they went, with a handful of eggs each, with Oscar squished in the middle and with two grins a mile wide.

For Athena and Nikos the day promised to be

far less exciting than the kids'. They needed to announce a coronation date, but first…there were so many papers to read and to sign that her head spun. The contracts and deeds ensuring legal ascension were mind-blowing.

But between the legal stuff, it was great that the kids were happy, she thought. She had visions of her son and Christa at Annia's kitchen table, where she'd spent the happiest part of her childhood. They were safe. And Nikos was right here, reading through the contracts with her, trying to make it less boring.

Her family was where it ought to be. She could cope with a boring day or two. And after she signed… Annia had offered to keep the children until dinner time. That meant Athena had a whole evening with Nikos, and no kids.

She was already thinking of the little cove under the castle. She'd have a secluded beach with only herself and Nikos.

She glanced up from the document she was signing and saw Nikos watching her—and she blushed.

He grinned.

She blushed some more.

She was signing the last contract. The lawyers were starting to pack up documents, beaming, congratulating.

And then Nikos's phone rang.

He listened and his face lost colour. She was at his side in an instant. 'What…what…'

'Mama's just rung,' he said. 'The kids… Demos has the kids.'

He had her hand. He was running, tugging her behind him, down the castle steps to the limousine parked in front. The lawyers were abandoned, shocked to silence.

She drove while Nikos barked orders into his phone. Then he told her what had happened.

'Mama used the time while she had the kids to cook dinner for a neighbour who's ill. The kids were playing—they were happy and she thought it'd only take five minutes to pop the food next door, the children were in the garden and Joe was in the house. He'd taken his eyes off the children only for a moment. The first he knew of trouble was a scream from the cove below the house. By the time he got down there they were gone.'

Gone…

'Is he sure it's Demos?' Athena asked in a voice she scarcely recognised as hers.

'He saw him,' he said, his voice catching. 'He had both the children in the boat—the same boat that tried to hit you. I've just rung Alexandros on Sappheiros. He has a helicopter. I thought this was safe. I never dreamed…' His voice broke.

She wanted to hold him. She had to keep driving, but it took every ounce of self-restraint not to pull over, take him in her arms and comfort him.

He was her man. She knew it. Whatever had happened in the past, Nikos was her man and she'd fight for him. As she'd fight for her child. Her children, she corrected herself. Her family.

CHAPTER ELEVEN

ANNIA was standing in her kitchen, white-faced and tearful. They walked in, she stepped straight into Nikos's arms and sobbed out her horror on his chest.

Then she tugged back from Nikos and hugged Athena. And then Joe came lumbering in, looking like a dog who'd been kicked. Before Thena knew it, Joe was a part of the hug.

Family.

Despite her terror, here was a glimmer of comfort. She let herself be hugged, she let herself be wept on and if she wept too, it didn't matter.

The hugs were fast; there were too many imperatives to indulge in emotion, but it steadied her. For this moment she'd take comfort where she could find it.

There were more men entering the kitchen

now, summoned by Joe—big men, determined, grave-faced. Not knowing what to do.

She held Nikos and Nikos held her. Who was holding who up? It didn't matter. They were facing this as one.

But there was nothing to do. The consensus was that all their hope had to be in Alexandros and his helicopter. It was the only thing fast enough to locate a boat so powerful.

She was trying so hard to think. How to think when you were enmeshed in panic? She must.

'What…what would Demos do with them?' she managed, speaking to the room in general, and the unsayable had been said.

Annia gave one heartrending sob and ended up held again by Nikos.

But Athena wasn't thinking like that. She met Nikos's gaze over his mother's head. She saw his terror, and inexplicably it steadied her.

She knew her cousin. He was a weak-willed man, greedy for riches. Desperate even. But he wasn't completely stupid.

'He wouldn't hurt them,' she said, and the words themselves steadied her, for she knew they were the truth. 'Not deliberately. Yes, he tried to kill Nicky and me, but that was aimed at the two of us, staged to be an accident. Think of all he'd lose by hurting them now. He's been seen. He knows that. If he's known to have hurt them, he could never claim this Crown. Plus, this world doesn't hold a hiding place deep and dark enough if he touches my Nicky.' She shook her head, still puzzled. 'And I don't understand how he got them both onto his boat. Was there only him?'

'Yes,' Joe said. 'He had them in the boat by the time I saw them.'

'If he'd grabbed Christa, Nicky might have decided to stay with her,' Nikos said doubtfully, following her train of thought. 'Was it Nicky who screamed?'

'It surely was,' Joe said. 'I heard him screaming from here, and by the time I reached the beach I could still hear him.'

'If Demos came up here and grabbed them…why didn't he scream here? You'd surely have heard if he had.'

Joe had no answers.

It made less and less sense. She knew her Nicky. 'For Demos to creep in here and grab them without alerting you… And to get him into the boat… Was he holding him? Why didn't he jump out?'

'I don't know. Maybe Demos tied him up. I couldn't see.'

'He'll be trying to blackmail you into giving up the throne,' Nikos said.

'He must be.' But she'd steadied. She'd heard enough now to be less panicked. 'And if he is then he'll contact us.' She forced herself to say what they all knew they had to do. 'We have to wait.'

But Nikos's face was still strained to breaking.

'Christa has a heart condition,' he said numbly to the room in general, and she felt his wash of absolute fear. Her normally daredevil lover was jelly in the face of a threat to his daughter. 'She's on medication. She has to have it. If we don't find her…'

'He can't have her,' Annia said fiercely. 'He'd never love her. Oh…'

'It's okay, Mama,' Nikos said, hauling himself together again in the face of his mother's terror. 'Demos doesn't want her and, like Thena said, he can't afford to hurt them. We'll find her.'

Oscar was at Thena's feet. She knelt and

hugged him while Nikos held his mother. 'Why didn't you bite him, Oscar?' she whispered.

There was no answer.

Her terror had faded a little. This had to be an attempt at blackmail, she thought. But…in her confused mind she found room for more questions. What had Annia said? *'He can't have her. He'd never love her.'*

Why would Demos want Christa? There were undercurrents here she didn't understand.

She straightened and Nikos's arm came round her waist and held. He was more afraid than she was, she thought.

How serious was Christa's heart condition?

Now wasn't the time to ask. Now it seemed all they could do was wait, and to wait seemed the hardest thing in the world.

'I'll make…I'll make coffee,' Annia said, but subsided into her handkerchief instead.

And then Nikos's phone rang.

He flipped it open and listened.

He had the absolute attention of everyone in the room. Even Oscar was looking up, though that probably had more to do with the time and the absence of dinner.

But Oscar's dinner was doomed to wait. Nikos flipped the phone closed again. Frowning.

'Alexandros himself is flying the chopper,' Nikos told them, speaking slowly, thinking it through as he spoke. 'That was Alex now. Demos and the children are indeed in the boat, and they seem fine. But, according to Alexandros, they're going nowhere. Their boat's stopped. He thinks it must have run out of petrol. It's floating half a mile off the northern end of the island. Alexandros is holding position until we can reach them.'

He took a deep breath. Moving on.

'We'll take my runabout. It's faster than the bigger boats,' he snapped. 'Let's go. I'll radio as soon as we know. Can you guys bring one of the bigger boats after us?'

He grabbed Athena's hand, and they were gone.

It took fifteen long minutes to get there. Fifteen minutes with the runabout's motor roaring at full throttle. Smashing through the swells with sickening thumps.

If Demos had restarted the engine… Or if they'd tipped the boat…

She glanced at Nikos and his face was grim as death.

He'd do whatever it took.

She'd never doubted it. Not for a minute. He'd do whatever he must to keep these children safe. To keep the islanders safe.

To keep her…

And suddenly her thoughts were lurching with the boat. Taking her beyond her present fear.

This man had betrayed her. Or she'd thought he had. But…as she watched him at the tiller, as she saw the bleakness behind his eyes, she felt the sense of betrayal finally leave her, and all that remained was the knowledge of his honour.

He'd lost his father when he was twelve. He'd been on the boat with him—his father had a heart attack and by the time twelve-year-old Nikos had managed to get their fishing boat back to harbour his father was dead.

From that day on he'd taken on responsibilities too heavy for a boy. He'd been desperate to care for everyone, to make sure nothing like his father's death happened again.

And Marika… Christa's mother. Nikos's short-term wife. She'd never been able to think of Marika without the pain of betrayal over-whelming her. But, given these moments of enforced thought, the scene they'd just left came back to her. And Annia's words, speaking of Christa.

'He can't have her,' Annia had said fiercely. *'He'd never love her.'*

Marika had been older than she was and a bit…reckless. She'd been infatuated by Demos, desperate to get away from her bully of a father and away from the island. Her mother was one of Nikos's relations—almost family—but her father was a thug. If her father had found out Marika was pregnant… She shuddered to think of his reaction.

The germ of an idea—the germ of truth she'd discovered back in Annia's kitchen—was suddenly turned to full blown certainty.

But now wasn't the time to be talking of this with Nikos. Nikos was sick with worry. She should be sick with worry too—but still things didn't quite fit. She knew her son.

He was very, very like his father.

Dare you…

Nicky knew who Demos was. He'd seen his portrait. He'd understood the threat from the boat.

And now the boat was stranded, according to Alexandros, floundering just outside the reef.

'They'll be okay,' she said, steadily and strongly, to Nikos, and Nikos looked back at her with despair.

'How can you know?'

'Because my son is resourceful and clever and brave,' she told him. 'Because my son will do whatever it takes. Because my son is just like his father.'

And there they were, right where Alexandros directed them. His helicopter was still hovering overhead.

As Alex had told them, there were three people in the boat. Demos. Christa. Nicky.

Demos was leaning over the side.

'He might be armed,' Nikos warned her as they approached but she looked ahead at her cousin and she shook her head.

'He's seasick.'

'He still might be dangerous.'

'You mean he might shoot me? Not Demos.' She shook her head scornfully. 'With Alexandros in the helicopter watching? With the entire

Argyros fishing fleet bearing down behind us? When he's totally occupied with his stomach?'

And she was right. Demos was beyond caring. They ran the runabout up beside the speedboat and he barely looked up at them.

Nikos had the two boats fastened together in seconds. He steadied, and then he lifted Christa over.

Thena took her and hugged her close, and Nicky clambered over himself and sat down in the middle and grinned at his mother and grinned at Nikos. He didn't look the least bit worried. He looked supremely pleased with himself.

'Hooray, you came. I knew my plan would work,' he said with smug satisfaction.

'You knew...' Nikos said faintly.

Other boats were approaching now. The bigger fishing boats were slower than Nikos's runabout, but the fishermen of Argyros had gunned their motors as fast as they could to be in the action.

There wasn't a lot of action. Demos was bent over the side. Their villain didn't look the least bit menacing.

The fishing boats were forming a circle. Even

if he got the motor going, there was no longer anywhere to run.

'He was all right until the motor stopped,' Nicky said scornfully, as they all looked at Demos. 'But as soon as it stopped, the boat started rolling up and down and up and down and…'

'Do you mind?' Athena said faintly. 'Not so much with the ups and downs. So can you take us back to dry land?' she asked, hugging Christa and looking a plea to Nikos.

Nikos hadn't heard. He was still watching Demos. But Demos was no longer a threat to anyone. He was a bundle of abject misery.

'Tell us what happened,' he said to Nicky, and the little boy's eyes gleamed. He was mischief personified. Just like his father.

'We saw him on the beach from Yia Yia's kitchen window,' he said, and the islander's word for Grandmama resonated with pride. Here, then, was another association Nicky was proud of. 'I knew it was him 'cos of the boat, and 'cos of the picture. He pulled the boat up on the beach, really fast into bushes and I knew he was trying to hide. Then he came up the cliff path. I said to Christa, I know how to stop his boat going again, so we snuck down the cove past the craypots and Joe didn't even see us going. And when we got to the boat it was just like the picture in the book—only it said sometimes the fuel tank's locked—but it wasn't so we opened it up and put a whole lot of sand in. But it was hard getting the top back on 'cos it got sandy and I just got it on when Demos came back. He saw me and tried to grab me but I ran away. But then he grabbed Christa. So I had to go with him.'

'Oh, Nicky…' Athena said, torn between pride and horror. 'You shouldn't have…'

'I couldn't let him just take Christa, could I?' he said, stung by implied criticism of such a great plan. 'She's my sister. He pushed her into the boat and he said he'd hurt her if I didn't come too, and I knew the sand was in the engine so I hopped in anyway. He said you had to agree to ab…to abdicate. He said he'd hurt me if you didn't. So I did get a little bit scared. I thought the boat would stop really fast or not go at all but it went for ages. It sounded sicker and sicker though, but then it stopped and *he* got sick. And he had a gun, but while he was sick I grabbed it from his belt and threw it into the water. And he tried to hit me but he started being sick again. And then the helicopter came and the man up there waved and I knew you'd come. So it was okay, wasn't it, Mama?'

'Yes,' she said and she found she was laughing. Through tears. Her son.

Her men.

And she looked at Nikos and on his face she saw a mixture of pride and love and hope…and awe. Awe, pure and simple.

And in that moment she knew what she had to do.

These were her men.

This was her family.

She was the Crown Princess of Argyros. It was up to her to claim them.

As dusk settled over the island they returned to the Palace. The Eagle's Nest was a hideaway for when there was a threat, but there was no longer a threat. And Athena knew—they all knew— that now was the time to lay claim to the throne so it could never be disputed.

Annia and Mrs Lavros took the children to be bathed and fed and put to bed. When Athena came downstairs it seemed half the men of Argyros had come to tie the threads together. Nikos and Alexandros were seated at the head of the long table in the ancient meeting room, where decisions on the rule of this island had been made for generation upon generation.

Nikos signalled that she sit between them. But she couldn't. Not yet. There were things she had to sort in her own mind first.

There were words she had to find. For now she'd leave the speaking to Nikos.

'We found the thugs who nearly killed the Princess Athena and Prince Nicholas.' Nikos was talking to everyone in the room, but he was watching her. 'They were guns-for-hire from Athens. Alexandros traced the boat, he found them, and we had the link we needed to Demos. But Demos obviously took fright. He's had an informer on the island. We know now who he is—a man my mother thought of as a friend, a man who forfeited that friendship for pay. He's already fled to Greece, but before he left he told Demos that today the children would be with my mother.'

The men in the room were silent. Shocked. As

was Nikos, Thena thought. He still looked gaunt—the terror of this afternoon would probably stay with him for ever—but he had himself in hand, her Prince of the People.

'We know it all now,' Nikos said, and managed a wry smile. 'It seems that seasickness is better than torture for getting information. The men who towed Demos to shore told him he'd stay in his boat until he told us everything, and now he has.'

'He wrote it down,' Alexandros added gravely. 'We handed him pen and paper and he wrote and signed a confession. Jail's looking pretty good to Demos. Anywhere where the ground's solid.'

He smiled, but Nikos didn't return the smile. The events of the day had shaken him too deeply for humour.

'He wasn't as unprepared as he seemed,' Nikos said heavily. 'He had a gun. Nicky described it to me, and…'

He broke off, his voice cracking. Alexandros put his hand on his friend's shoulder and Athena thought blindly, these two men cared deeply for each other.

Her mind steadied. Focused. Knew what had to be done.

'Enough,' Nikos said and forced himself to go on. 'So… Demos beached the boat, he went up to the cottage and found no one. He returned to the boat—furious—to find the children, seemingly waiting for him.'

He hesitated, and Thena could see him repress a shudder. 'Maybe…maybe that was the best thing that could have happened. For if Joe had been in the garden and Annia had been at home…there could well have been a bloodbath as he seized Nicky and decided to eliminate witnesses.' He closed his eyes.

Alexandros took over. 'We know now that Demos has a king-sized gambling problem,' he added. 'He's been gambling on the assumption he'd have access to all the Argyros diamond mines. He was desperate enough to do anything to get his hands on that stream of wealth.'

Athena shivered. She was standing by the door, leaning against the wall. She'd said she wanted to be able to leave easily if the kids needed her. But in reality she just needed to watch, listen and figure what had to be said. And how she was going to say it.

'So he's in jail,' Alexandros said, and glanced

across at Athena. 'If it's okay by you, Princess Athena, I'll take care of him on Sappheiros.'

The men were all watching her now. Waiting for her to speak. She took a deep breath. She looked at Nikos's haggard face. She knew what had to be said.

'Thank you for your offer, Alexandros,' she said, forcing her voice to be steady. Forcing her words to be clear enough to be heard the length of the great room. 'But Demos will be tried here. We'd be thankful if you'd hold him for us until we have the facilities for a full and fair trial. But Prince Nikos and I will build this island's court system as one of our earliest priorities.'

'Prince Nikos,' Alexandros said blankly.

'Prince Nikos,' she repeated.

'If you abdicate, Nikos can't…' he began.

'I have no intention of abdicating.'

Maybe she should have dressed in her royal gear again, she thought. She'd dressed neatly this morning, for the lawyers, in smart casual trousers and a crisp white blouse. But since then she'd been hammered by the sea. Oscar had jumped up on her when they'd docked and she was covered in sand. Her hair was a wild tangle from the wind. She'd abandoned her soaked shoes and she was still barefoot—and she didn't care.

She was Crown Princess Athena and it was time for her to claim what was hers.

'Ten years ago Nikos Andreadis asked me to marry him,' she said, and she left the relative obscurity of her alcove near the door and walked deliberately around the table to its head. She stood between the two men—the two princes—and she looked out over the men of power from this island. Her people.

'Ten years ago there were misunderstandings and threats,' she said. 'I left this island because I believed harm would come to it's people if I stayed. Nikos let me go because he thought I was intent on a career. For ten years there's been misunderstanding and grief. But no more. This day is a watershed for this island. This day I say to you all—to the entire island—that I'm here to stay. That ten years ago Nikos asked me to marry me. I accepted his offer, and now, if he'll have me, I'd like to hold him to that contract. I would like Nikos and I to rule this island as man and wife. Prince Nikos and Princess Athena of Argyros.'

She turned and looked at Nikos. Who was looking…stunned.

'Nikos, you're a man of honour,' she said. 'I know—we all know—that you would never ask me to marry you if there was a hint that your offer would be taken as a desire to rule this island yourself. Everyone in this room knows you're an honourable man. Everyone in this room knows the island is your home, your heart. Is there any man in this room who would say Prince Nikos shouldn't take what I see as his rightful role? As ruler beside me?'

There wasn't a sound. Not a sound.

Nikos was staring at her blindly, as if he couldn't believe what she'd just said. The silence stretched on and on.

And then one lone person, far up the back of the long hall, started to clap. And then another started beside him. And then another.

And then the whole room was clapping. They were on their feet, cheering, shouting, clapping each other on the back.

And Nikos was simply staring at Athena. Saying nothing.

The applause died. Athena watched the men regain their seats.

Still Nikos said nothing.

'I believe,' she said softly into the silence, 'that you'll have to excuse us. Nikos and I have a few things to discuss.'

There was a delighted roar of laughter. Nikos was looking as thrown as a man could be, and their audience was loving it.

'So can we call this meeting closed?' she said. 'I think we've achieved everything we wished for. Oh, and when the council next meets... I want this room to hold at least as many women as it does men.'

'You'll be under petticoat rule now,' someone called to Nikos.

'And he'll love it,' someone else called.

'Our Princess isn't one for petticoats as far as I can see,' someone else added. 'I'm thinking climbing trees and saving kids and making us proud of her is where she is. That's where they both are. Our royal couple.'

But Athena wasn't listening. She was watching Nikos.

'Well?' she said softly. 'How about the beach? Is it private enough? Or should we go back to our sky dome?'

'Thena…'

'Your call, but we have to talk,' she said, and he stared at her for a long moment—and then he smiled, that wonderful heart-twisting smile she loved so much. He rose and he took her hand.

And the men of the island council rose again and cheered as one, as the people's Prince led his Princess from the room.

CHAPTER TWELVE

THEY didn't need to go far. Just as far as the cliff path, where they could look out on the rising moon, the moonbeams glittering over the ocean, where there was only silence and each other.

'What have you done?' Nikos asked gently, and Athena smiled because she knew that even now he'd be honourable.

'I've claimed my own.'

'You don't need to marry me to be a princess.'

'I never did,' she said. 'But I do need to marry you because I love you and I need you by my side.'

He took a deep breath. He turned to face her and he took both her hands in his.

'Thena, I hurt you…'

'So you did,' she said. 'And I hurt you. It's in the past.'

'But you explained…'

'And you can't.' She hesitated, but it had to be said. Once and then never again.

'Nikos, when I left the island… You know I went hoping you'd follow. I knew you'd be hurt but I hoped…I hoped so much that I could explain my reasons for leaving. But then I found I was pregnant. And, while I was working up the courage to phone you, I was told that Marika was pregnant. And that you'd promised to marry her. And that she was further gone in her pregnancy than I was.'

He groaned.

All she wanted to do was hold him—kiss him—but this had to be said. She had to sort this in her head. Get it right.

'So I thought you'd betrayed me,' she said softly. 'Until today…'

'So what's happened today?' he demanded in a voice she hardly recognised. 'To make you change your mind.'

And somehow she found the strength and certainty to answer.

'When Annia said: *"He can't have her. He'd never love her,"* I knew then what had happened. I knew.'

'How can you know? No one…'

'No one will ever know from me,' she whispered. 'You know, and Annia knows—or maybe she's just guessing as well. But when I left the island I was heartbroken, and I can only imagine how you must have felt. Maybe, given time, you'd have contacted me, seen how things really were. But along came Marika. Sure, I'm guessing, but I know I'm right. I'm guessing Marika came begging for your help. Pregnant by Demos. Abandoned by Demos. Terrified that her bully of a father might well kill her if he found out.'

She couldn't bear to watch him. She couldn't bear to see the pain. Nikos said nothing but the bleakness in his eyes told her all she'd ever want to know. She was speaking the truth.

'So I'm guessing you thought why not? You thought I'd betrayed you and abandoned the island, so why not help Marika? So you went with Marika to her parents and said yes, Marika's pregnant, but the two of you wanted to marry. Instead of being appalled, her father would have welcomed you with open arms. So you married.

'But then a baby was born,' she whispered. 'A little girl with Down's syndrome. A child who Demos would never have cared for. Marika herself obviously couldn't cope and she chose to run.'

Still he said nothing. His silence was frightening her. But she'd come this far—there was no choice but to take it to its conclusion.

'But you…' she said, and she knew in her heart that she spoke the absolute truth. 'You stood with Christa in your arms and you declared to all the island that she was yours. With the respect you and your mother are held on this island, affection for Christa is guaranteed. She has Annia as a grandmama. She has you as her papa. She's safe.'

And at last he broke his silence. 'You're just guessing,' he said explosively.

'So tell me I'm wrong. Look at me straight, Nikos and tell me I'm wrong.'

He didn't. He couldn't. The pain that had wrapped itself around her heart ten long years ago dissolved and faded to nothing.

He'd do…*whatever it took.*

Her Prince. Her Nikos.

'I'll never ask you to confirm it,' she said softly,

seeing raw pain. 'But I know I'm right.' She forced a rueful smile. 'Christa is your daughter. She stays your daughter, no matter what else happens. My only regret is that I've been so stupid. A bit of terror and fifteen minutes in an open boat and I've guessed it all. Oh, Nikos, I love what you did. I love what you are.' She hesitated then, but she'd come so far… Why not go on.

'So…I know it's not the woman who's supposed to say these things,' she whispered. 'But your honour won't let you. So here it is. Nikos, I'm saying, right here, right now, that I love you with all my heart. That if you demand it of me, then I'll rule this island alone, but only if you refuse what I'm asking. Because it seems to me that we've had ten years alone and why wait one minute longer? You asked me to marry you ten years ago and I accepted. Only then Giorgos destroyed it. So today I've accepted again, in front of the full island council. And I accept again now.'

His hands were tight on hers. His face was expressionless again, but she knew what that meant. It meant he was hiding what he felt. She knew this man as she knew herself.

'I love you, Nikos,' she whispered. 'I've loved you since I was eight years old and I love you still. If you want me to be your wife, it would be an honour and it would be my joy to accept.'

'If I want you,' he whispered.

'So?' she said, and tilted her chin and even managed a smile. 'So, Nikos Andreadis? Prince of my heart. Dare you.'

'Dare to marry you?'

'I'll make a very demanding wife,' she whispered, venturing a smile. 'Plus I have it on the best authority that I snortle.'

'I love your snortle.'

'I don't snortle.'

'I believe you just said…'

'Nikos!'

'I like to get my facts right,' he said, mischief emerging, the wicked grin that had her heart doing handsprings causing its normal damage again—and more. 'I need to let myself know what I'm getting into,' he said. 'One wife?'

'Only one,' she said. 'No Henry the Eighth absurdity for this royal couple.'

'Agreed,' he said promptly.

'One son?'

'And one daughter,' she said serenely. 'And…and maybe even more?' And his answering smile was enough to make her heart turn over.

'I guess you'll expect me to adopt Oscar as well,' he said, struggling for a martyred tone.

'Of course I will.'

'So…'

'So?' she whispered and held her breath.

'So,' he said and dropped to his knee before her.

She gasped. 'Nikos…'

'So let's get this right,' he said softly. 'As my Princess, to whom I owe fidelity and all honour, you've asked me to marry you.'

'Yes,' she said, suddenly doubtful. 'But it doesn't mean you must.'

'No, but there are connotations of duty to my Crown Princess,' he said. 'And I'd hate you to think I'd just said yes to stop myself being thrown in a dungeon.'

'Do we have dungeons?'

'We'll find out together,' he whispered. 'Meanwhile, Princess Athena Christou of Argyros, would you let me get a word in edgeways?'

'Yes,' she said—and did.

'Will you do me the great honour of becoming my wife?'

'Of course I will,' she said, and tugged him up to stand before her. 'If you really want me.'

'How can you ask?'

'I'll never ask again,' she whispered. 'I'll never need to ask again. Oh, Nikos. My one and only love.'

'My Thena,' he whispered into her hair. 'My Princess and my life.'

And then he put her away from him. He held her at arm's length and his face broke into a smile she'd never seen before. It was a look of exultation, triumph and pride. 'My Thena.' It was a shout of pure joy and it echoed down into the cove below, back into the palace behind them, out onto the sea breezes blowing over the whole island.

He swung her round and round and round, and then he set her down before him and he kissed her, long and hard and true.

And then, finally, he set her back from him again.

He held her hands and he held her heart.

'Thena, I've loved you for ever,' he said softly. 'So…you'll really be my wife?'

'Yes.'

'Princess to my Prince?'

'Absolutely.'

'Mama to my Papa?'

'That, too.'

'My lover?'

'You're very demanding.'

'You have no idea how demanding,' he said. His hands were tugging her into him, his eyes were dark and fathomless and she was against his heart, held tight, his hand cupping her chin so her mouth was just under his.

'We're family,' he said fiercely, and it was as if he was making a vow. 'You'll be my wife and I'll not let you go again. I love you Athena. I've loved you since I was eight years old and I don't intend stopping until I'm a hundred and eight. Or longer if I'm granted more years by your side.'

'Stupid,' she said softly, lovingly, and as an echo to a vow it was pretty dumb—but it didn't matter.

She was kissing him.

He was kissing her back.

And, on the steps of the Royal Palace of

Argyros, half the island council and practically all the palace staff were craning their heads to see.

The island had its royal family.

And the Prince and his Princess didn't notice their audience at all.

The combined wedding and coronation of the Crown Prince and Crown Princess of Argyros was a day to remember for ever. The sun shone gently on the rugged cliffs and distant mountains. The ocean glittered in its sapphire and diamond brilliance. The warm breeze from the sea was almost a caress.

Coronations and royal weddings should take place in a formal setting—most properly in the Great Hall of the Royal Palace. That was a problem, for the Great Hall only held five hundred, and all the island wanted to see.

So they held the ceremony on the wide sweep of lawn between the palace and what had once been the most private of beaches. No invitation was necessary. Whosoever loved this island and wished it well was welcome, to see the beginning of its future.

And its future was assured. In the best of monarchies, the royal family was an embodiment of the hopes and dreams of the people and, in Nikos and Athena, the islanders of Argyros had found that dream.

Nikos, in royal uniform—jet-black jacket and trousers, shining boots, tassels, braid, dress sword—was eye-candy enough to have at least half their audience sighing with pure enchantment. And Athena, in her clouds of swirling silk and lace, was a bride to turn the most hardened islander misty-eyed. She made her vows clearly and solemnly and she looked so happy there was hardly a dry eye on the island.

Even Father Antonio… The old priest married them with love and with pride, and there was definitely a tear or two rolling down his wrinkled cheek. As he blessed the bride and groom, his old voice became redolent with joy.

His blessing was supposed to be just for the bride and groom—the Prince and Princess—but he didn't stop there. He blessed the ancient ring on Athena's finger, the ring of Argyros, ancient silver, gnarled and twisted and lovely, with three magnificent diamonds embedded in its depths. He blessed the islanders looking on. He blessed

Alexandros and Lily from the Isle of Sappheiros. And he blessed Stefanos, even now trying to sort the future of the third and last island.

And of course he blessed the children. Nicky was pageboy, torn a little between embarrassment and pride. Pride was definitely winning. Christa was flower girl, with so many pink and white flounces she'd announced that any minute now she might float. Indulging her fancy, the dressmaker had attached a tiny pair of gossamer wings to her back. Christa's happiness was complete. She had a mama and a papa, a brother and a dog. And wings. She was tossing her rose petals with delight, and she was making Nicky toss them with her.

Two royal children…and even now the island grandmothers were dusting off their knitting needles in hope.

But knitting was for the future. Everything was for the future. For now the royal couple knelt to receive the ancient crowns that had lain in storage for over two hundred years. They rose to thunderous applause.

To a happy beginning.

* * *

Crown Princess Athena and Crown Prince Nikos stood hand in hand on the raised dais and looked out on the island of their birth, and if there were tears shed in the crowd then the islanders' tears found reflection in the face of the new Crown Princess of Argyros.

The Crown was secure. The Argyros diamonds were confirmed as belonging to the people, and legal proceedings were already underway to ensure no royal held such terrifying powers again.

Demos was stripped of his title and waiting for the courts to administer justice. Exile, Athena thought, for there was room in her heart to almost feel sorry for the man.

So what was next?

It had been leaked by the media that Prince Nikos had decreed a month's honeymoon was the minimum required to cement their union. The islanders, deliriously happy at their good fortune, could only smile their agreement.

Nikos had offered his wife any place in the world for their time out. A deserted island in the Maldives, a tropical *bure*, nights alone by candlelight...

She'd chosen...the Eagle's Nest. They'd leave

for there tonight. With Nicky and with Christa and with Oscar.

'For I have a daughter now,' she'd whispered proudly to Nikos.

He'd held her close, he'd kissed her eyelids and he'd felt so much in love that surely his heart must burst.

They'd face the future together, he thought, and if the worst happened... They were a family. They'd face their future with love and with courage.

And with a dog called Oscar. And with a grandmother called Annia. And uncles and aunts and cousins. And thousands of islanders who loved this place as they did.

Their island home.

'It's perfect,' he whispered to Athena as they stood side by side and waved to the assembled population of Argyros. 'I can't imagine anything more perfect than this.'

'I can't imagine anyone more perfect than you,' she whispered back.

'Then you need to look in the mirror,' he retorted, and then this very serious ceremonial occasion was marred.

This ceremony had been timed to the last nano-second. There was no room for improvisation. Right now the Crown Prince was supposed to take the Crown Princess's hand and solemnly lead her to the pair of gold and crimson thrones at the middle of the crimson-carpeted dais.

He didn't.

Instead, for three whole minutes—for one whole trumpet chorale that was supposed to see them taking the throne together—the Crown Prince of Argyros took the Crown Princess of Argyros into his arms and he kissed her.

As he intended to kiss her for the rest of her life.

MILLS & BOON PUBLISH EIGHT LARGE PRINT TITLES A MONTH. THESE ARE THE EIGHT TITLES FOR FEBRUARY 2010.

DESERT PRINCE, BRIDE OF INNOCENCE
Lynne Graham

RAFFAELE: TAMING HIS TEMPESTUOUS VIRGIN
Sandra Marton

THE ITALIAN BILLIONAIRE'S SECRETARY MISTRESS
Sharon Kendrick

BRIDE, BOUGHT AND PAID FOR
Helen Bianchin

BETROTHED: TO THE PEOPLE'S PRINCE
Marion Lennox

THE BRIDESMAID'S BABY
Barbara Hannay

THE GREEK'S LONG-LOST SON
Rebecca Winters

HIS HOUSEKEEPER BRIDE
Melissa James

MILLS & BOON PUBLISH EIGHT LARGE PRINT TITLES A MONTH. THESE ARE THE EIGHT TITLES FOR MARCH 2010.

A BRIDE FOR HIS MAJESTY'S PLEASURE
Penny Jordan

THE MASTER PLAYER
Emma Darcy

THE INFAMOUS ITALIAN'S SECRET BABY
Carole Mortimer

THE MILLIONAIRE'S CHRISTMAS WIFE
Helen Brooks

CROWNED: THE PALACE NANNY
Marion Lennox

CHRISTMAS ANGEL FOR THE BILLIONAIRE
Liz Fielding

UNDER THE BOSS'S MISTLETOE
Jessica Hart

JINGLE-BELL BABY
Linda Goodnight

millsandboon.co.uk Community

Join Us!

The Community is the perfect place to meet and chat to kindred spirits who love books and reading as much as you do, but it's also the place to:

- **Get the inside scoop from authors about their latest books**
- **Learn how to write a romance book with advice from our editors**
- **Help us to continue publishing the best in women's fiction**
- **Share your thoughts on the books we publish**
- **Befriend other users**

Forums: Interact with each other as well as authors, editors and a whole host of other users worldwide.

Blogs: Every registered community member has their own blog to tell the world what they're up to and what's on their mind.

Book Challenge: We're aiming to read 5,000 books and have joined forces with The Reading Agency in our inaugural Book Challenge.

Profile Page: Showcase yourself and keep a record of your recent community activity.

Social Networking: We've added buttons at the end of every post to share via digg, Facebook, Google, Yahoo, technorati and de.licio.us.

www.millsandboon.co.uk

0909/COMMUNITY LP